BARNABY

LECTOR HOUSE PUBLIC DOMAIN WORKS

This book is a result of an effort made by Lector House towards making a contribution to the preservation and repair of original classic literature. The original text is in the public domain in the United States of America, and possibly other countries depending upon their specific copyright laws.

In an attempt to preserve, improve and recreate the original content, certain conventional norms with regard to typographical mistakes, hyphenations, punctuations and/or other related subject matters, have been corrected upon our consideration. However, few such imperfections might not have been rectified as they were inherited and preserved from the original content to maintain the authenticity and construct, relevant to the work. The work might contain a few prior copyright references as well as page references which have been retained, wherever considered relevant to the part of the construct. We believe that this work holds historical, cultural and/or intellectual importance in the literary works community, therefore despite the oddities, we accounted the work for print as a part of our continuing effort towards preservation of literary work and our contribution towards the development of the society as a whole, driven by our beliefs.

We are grateful to our readers for putting their faith in us and accepting our imperfections with regard to preservation of the historical content. We shall strive hard to meet up to the expectations to improve further to provide an enriching reading experience.

Though, we conduct extensive research in ascertaining the status of copyright before redeveloping a version of the content, in rare cases, a classic work might be incorrectly marked as not-in-copyright. In such cases, if you are the copyright holder, then kindly contact us or write to us, and we shall get back to you with an immediate course of action.

HAPPY READING!

BARNABY

RINA RAMSAY

ISBN: 978-93-90294-39-8

Published: 1910

© 2020
LECTOR HOUSE LLP

LECTOR HOUSE LLP
E-MAIL: lectorpublishing@gmail.com

BARNABY
A NOVEL
BY

R. RAMSAY
AUTHOR OF "THE KEY OF THE DOOR," "THE STRAW," ETC.

1910

TO
THE MEMORY OF
MY FATHER

CONTENTS

Page

1. CHAPTER I 1
2. CHAPTER II 6
3. CHAPTER III 16
4. CHAPTER IV 25
5. CHAPTER V 37
6. CHAPTER VI 48
7. CHAPTER VII 58
8. CHAPTER VIII 73
9. CHAPTER IX 84
10. CHAPTER X 90
11. CHAPTER XI 98
12. CHAPTER XII 109
13. CHAPTER XIII 119
14. CHAPTER XIV 130

BARNABY

CHAPTER I

The lamp flickered and jumped at the stamping in the bar.

There was a frantic quality in that noise, laughter and exclamation mixed with a wild shouting that made the crazy partition quiver. It was a mad reaction from the common weight of despair.

From the bed in the room behind you could watch the door....

Paradise Town was a broken link in the chain of civilization; it might have been written in letters of rusted blood on the map. Its pioneers had forsaken it cursing, its trees had been burned for firewood, its earth had been riddled in vain for gold. All that was left of it was huddled near the shanty where men could buy drink and blur the spell of awful loneliness that shut them away from life. It was worse at night. With the darkness fell a heavier sense of the distance of human help, and Paradise was an island in a black sea of haunted land. East and west, wide and silent, the unknown emptiness lapped it in.

Ill-luck and some bitter trick had stranded the M'Kune Tragedy Company in this dreadful place. Night after night they played in a shingle hut with their useless scenery stacked outside; night after night M'Kune broke it to his scared company that they hadn't yet got their fares. Fear and a kind of superstition worked in their minds until they were seized with panic. In the daylight the men hung about the bar, muttering; and the women herded by themselves, packed like hens in a strange run, hysterically afraid. Prisoners in a desert, when night had fallen they wandered away to the railroad track and watched. Towards midnight would rise a red gleam on the far horizon, and they would hear a distant rumbling, gathering to a roar, till the darkness was split by a whizzing bar of light. By it went, the great, glaring thing full of life, terrible in its rush, and leaving the night immeasurably darker. Among the watchers the men would affect to whistle. If they couldn't board her to-night they might manage it to-morrow.... But the women caught each other's hands fast, and shuddered. Latterly they had felt as if the train were a devil that counted and kept them there.

But their desperate plight inspired them. Never in their lives had these poor mummers so hurled themselves into their parts; never again would they murder and cheat and punish with such passionate realism. Their fate hung upon it. Penniless and trapped, their solitary chance of rescue lay in witching all Paradise to stare at them and furnish the wherewithal.

"Keep it up," urged M'Kune when a tired actress flagged. The hut was full and airless, but a few men were sullenly hanging back in the doorway, drawn thither, but arguing if it was worth it to step inside. "Keep it up!" hissed M'Kune.

And the heroine flung herself between the hero and the villain's knife, slipped as she ran, and was hurt, but struggled up and cried out her tottering defiance, bringing the house down before she dropped on her face.

That was the last night of crazed endeavour. The curtain came rocking down, and the villain—M'Kune—cheated the gallows to run feverishly through his receipts. All Paradise was vociferating behind that flapping rag, but amidst the din the players had heard their manager's yell of triumph. They had made up their fares at last.

The Tragedy Company scattered and fled, each in search of his own belongings; but they had little to gather, and the night wind blew them together like drifting leaves. They durst not squander their means of escaping, durst not loiter. The train, thundering by in its midnight passage, must lift them out of this nightmare town. Waiting they filled the bar, singing and shouting like lunatics, beside themselves with joy.

The door in the partition rattled, but stayed shut, and on the inner side was silence. Nobody lifted the latch, though the bursts of noise shook it from time to time. A selfish panic had left no room for any other feeling. Probably they had all forgotten that one of the Tragedy Company who could not escape out of Paradise; and it was all in vain that the crazy bedstead was turned in its corner to face the door.

She lay without moving. It seemed as if there were nothing of her but the long black hair covering the pillow. In their hurry those who had carried her in had not taken out all the pins, and a few glistened in it still. Looking closer, one saw that her hands were clenched tight against her breast, as if to keep her heart quiet.

How fast the minutes went! It must be nearly train time. And surely there was a vast thing, pulsing, pulsing, like an engine, far away in the night? She could bear the hubbub of voices, but not the dread of silence. Was it quite impossible to rise up and struggle to them, and reach a human face? ... Suddenly she took a panting breath, short like a sob, still gazing.

The door had opened at last, and a woman looked in hastily, and, flinging a word over her shoulder to the rest, stepped forward, shutting out the streak of light and the voices in the bar. Then she paused, irresolute. It was so dim in here, the atmosphere was so anxious.... And nothing stirring ... just a glimmer of wild black hair.

"You poor little thing!" she said.

Her voice was warm with the cheap kindness of a nature tuned to play with emotion, but incapable of feeling it from within. Her sympathy smacked of the stage, but as far as it went was ready to proffer easy help.

"Like the Flight out of Egypt, isn't it?" she said. "It's a shame to leave you behind. If M'Kune would hear reason, and any of us had a cent to spare, I'd make a

CHAPTER I

bundle of you, and carry you on to the train myself. But it won't run to it. I asked him. We're nothing but ranting beggars.... You'd better write to your friends."

The girl on the bed laughed.

So much of despair betrayed itself in that tragic note that the woman was startled. She came a little nearer.

"You don't mean it's as bad as that?" she said, lower. "All dead?—I might have known it. They wouldn't have let a thing like you fling about with us. But you'll be all right; you'll rub along somehow. We all do.... And that man who was once a doctor—"

But at her words a quick terror came to drive out the girl's submission to despair. She threw out her hands, clutching at the other woman's dress.

"What?" said she, comprehending. "Then the brute's charity and promising to M'Kune—Oh, Lord, what a horrible place it is— —!"

"Don't go!" The girl's voice was a choking cry.

The woman swung round and listened. Were the rest starting already? Her fine eyes darkened. She was wrapped up for the night journey in a faded crimson cloak, her usual wear in tragedy, alike as empress and villainess. Its dull glow warmed a beauty that was, like her soul, not quite real. Perhaps she was repenting the hasty impulse that had brought her in. But she could not pull herself loose from that piteous hold.

The younger one looked up beseechingly in her face. Her spirit failed her; she hardly knew what an impracticable thing she was asking, how uselessly she was clinging, in her horror of friendlessness.

"I'm so frightened ... I'm so frightened..." she whispered, panting because the effort hurt her; her lips were pale, and her forehead was damp with pain.

Suddenly the woman clapped her hands.

"I've got it!" she said. Her face cleared, and she began to laugh like one whose mind was rid of a burden. Twisting a ring off her finger, she caught the little desperate hand still clutching at her skirt, and thrust the ring on.

"There!" she said. "Change with me."

"I can't understand," said the girl faintly. The other woman burst into vehement explanation.

"It's Providence!" she said. "Never tell me—! I'm used to this life with its ups and downs, and its glitter of luck ahead. It's in my bones; the restlessness, and all that. I couldn't give it up. I wouldn't. But you—! You didn't guess there was a lawyer tracking me, did you?—that I'm a widow?—that I'm wanted to go and live in England with his mother. Perhaps she'd have to pay somebody if I hadn't a sense of duty.... *Me* picking up stitches in her knitting, yawning in a parlour with a parrot!—But you'd be safe there, you child—!"

She paused for breath, triumphant.

"I'll tell him to fetch you," she said. "The lawyer. Wait a minute—I have his letter; warning me that there is no money in it—no settlements, as he calls it. I'd be depending on the old woman's chanty, like any stray cat."

She went down immediately on her knees, and plunged into a kit-bag that she had slung on her arm, turning out its miscellaneous load. There was a shiver of glass as she fumbled, spilling things right and left; and the stale air was scented with heliotrope.

"That's all you want," she said, throwing a heap of papers on the bed. "Here's his photograph. You can have it. I can't tell you much about him, but you'll find the clues in there. He was good-looking, too, poor fellow; a great gawk of a good-for-nothing working with his hands. John Barnabas Hill—the boys called him Lord John among themselves, and persuaded me he was incognito. But when I asked him after the wedding if I was now my lady, he just laughed and laughed; and I went right off in a passion and never saw him again. It wasn't his fault. I was just too eager; that's all there was to it. And I'll tell the lawyer I've left you ill in this wilderness. He'll rush to your side, and take it for granted that you are me. Don't look so scared. What's the matter?"

"I can't do it," the girl panted, staring with a dizzy wonder at the casual Samaritan on her knees. Surely the lamp was sinking, the darkness seemed dangerously near, the kneeling figure brilliant in a blur. She tried to keep a picture of that kind human face wherewith to fill the darkness, while instinctively repudiating her mad suggestion.

"Rubbish!" said the woman. "It's the simplest thing. You do nothing.—And you're an actress."

"But I cannot," the girl said over and over again, holding fast.

"You'll hurt nobody," urged the woman, attaining to some imperfect apprehension of an attitude of mind that would not, even in extremity, buy help with falsehood. "If I'm willing to have you stand in my shoes, who else has a right to grumble? It's perfectly fair all round. Look! I'm stuffing these papers under your pillow. I'll tell them all outside that an English lawyer is coming for you, and that'll make things easy. Don't hinder me leaving you with a clear conscience. I've been your friend, haven't I? Hush, hush! I tell you you must.... I'll not let you die in this den. I'll not be haunted——!"

There was a tramping in the bar without. They were going. She tumbled her belongings into the bag, and clapped it shut. The rest of them were calling her.

"Luck!" she said, "and good-bye."

Her eyes dimmed unexpectedly, and she bent in a shamefaced hurry, printing a kiss on the girl's cheek ... and fled.

The door closed. In imagination one might see the midnight train thundering towards the watchers—hear the grinding of the brakes. To the bustle had succeeded a dreadful stillness. They had all gone like shadows, and the listener was deserted.

CHAPTER I

"I can't ... I can't ... I can't!" she reiterated in a sobbing whisper, casting the strange chance from her with a last effort of consciousness. The lamp was dying, and the world seemed to be turning round. In that unfriended darkness the ring on her finger was glittering like a charm.

CHAPTER II

The day's hunting was over.

Of the hundreds who had jostled each other in the first run, a disreputable few survived, pulling up after that last gallop. They grinned contentedly, drawing out their watches. Thirty-five minutes from the wood; a straight fox and elbow-room. It had been worth stopping out for, though now the dusk was thickening fast, and the huntsman was calling off his hounds.

"Where's Rackham?" asked one man, peering into the hollow.

"Gone home. I saw his back as we came through Pickwell."

"That wasn't Rackham. That was Bond, hurrying home to tea."

"He's probably come to grief. His horse had had about enough when I lost him."

Another man popped his head over the hedge that had worsted him. His hat was stove in, and his tired animal was blowing on the farther side.

"*He's* all right," he said. "The devil looks after his own. I turned the most horrible somersault back yonder, through my horse catching his leg in a binder; and before I could pick myself up, over shoots Rackham, practically on the top of us. If he'd even given me time to roll into the ditch!—Down he went to the water.... I wish I could think he was swimming in it."

"He's not far, anyhow. Hark to him. I'd know that laugh of his a mile off. There he goes—'Haw, haw, haw!'—all by himself, in the valley."

They turned their heads to listen, with a broadening and sympathetic grin, as the dim outline of a horseman took shape in the semi-obscurity, travelling upwards. It wasn't at all unlike Rackham to turn up like that, though there hadn't been a sign of him till they heard his laughter. The wonder would have been if he had let himself be beaten altogether. What obstinacy had kept him going was explained by the spur marks on his horse's sides as he brushed through a gap and took stock of the diminished party, the handful that had, by a minute or two, outstripped him.

"Only the tough 'uns in it," he said. "It wasn't bad. Has the fox dipped into the sunset and left you staring? Where are we? We must feel our way home, or let the horses smell it out."

"He's run into a drain. The usual end. What was the joke?" asked the nearest man. Rackham pulled out his yellow silk handkerchief, and twisted it round his

CHAPTER II

throat. He was hot, and the air was clammy. With that, and his wild eyes, and his sandy moustache, he looked like a handsome bandit.

"It's turning cold," he said. "What? Didn't you hear the plaintive toot of a motor lying in wait for the man who sells pills? I'm morally certain the millionaire is feebly chasing his hunter round and round that big field with the mole-hills in it, miles and miles behind. I suppose the chauffeur had his orders; but it would be a charity to hint that following hounds is the worst way to pick up his master."

"Didn't somebody catch his horse?"

"Oh, I did, and chucked him the reins; but I didn't see him get on to him. I'll bet the idiot let him go."

"Do him good. He'll probably sit on a gate and pass the time inventing another pill."

"Awful if he's benighted, and all the ghosts of all who swallowed the other pills pop up screeching— —!"

"Poor devil; he will have a time of it, with the mole-hills and the thistles, and all those ghosts."

The picture called up was upsetting to the general gravity, and they dispersed, chuckling in the increasing twilight. A division made for the turnpike, with here and there an individual branching courageously into a bridle road; and the larger half halted under a signpost that stretched illegible arms east and west in the lane. It was pleasant to linger a minute or two, lighting up, guessing at their direction. But Rackham kept on.

"That's not your way, Rackham," one man called after him.

The match flickered at his cigar, and went out as he threw it in the road. His horse was walking on with his head down, guided by the rider's knees.

"Right," he shouted back. "It isn't. Is that you, Parsley? I nearly jumped on you, didn't I?"

"You did," said one of the dawdling group. "He has been complaining."

"Well, if a fellow will sit down unexpectedly before you, like a hen under a motor, how can you dodge him? Teach that lazy brute of yours to lift up his hind legs, Parsley. Do you never hit him?"

"I say," called the first man. "Come back. Where are you going?" But Rackham pursued his wrong road untroubled.

"He can make Melton that way, if he likes," said one of those who were looking after him. "I daresay he means to call in on Lady Henrietta. He told me he had a message from her, asking him to come over, but he wasn't going to miss a day's hunting to see what she was up to."

"I thought they were at daggers drawn."

"In a manner of speaking," said the first, dropping his voice a little; "but outwardly they are civil. Of course, she hates him coming in for poor Barnaby's property, and I know he was at the bottom of that row that made Barnaby rush abroad."

"Ah, I remember, Rackham flirted furiously with Julia— —"

They edged instinctively nearer to each other, snatching at an enlivening bit of gossip as they jogged on together with the bats swooping overhead.

"No mistake about that. And she let Barnaby see plainly that she was ready to drop her bone for—his cousin. Of course, Rackham is a bigger match. She's one of these women who can't perceive that titles are getting vulgar."

"Rum chap, Rackham. I can't quite make him out. What did he do it for?"

"He owed Barnaby one, perhaps. I don't think he was fond of Julia. Anyhow, he didn't rise to her expectations; and so she relapsed, and repented, and trails about now like a mourning bride. Poor old Barnaby; he'll be missed.... And we'll never hear what wild things he did out there."

"Desperate sort of cure, to disappear in the backwoods, and never call on his bankers. Just like him though.—But he shouldn't have got himself killed in a scuffle in some outlandish quarter, and spoilt the yarn."

The man next him grunted.

"Who started the rumour that it wasn't an accident," he inquired; "but that life without Julia wasn't worth tuppence to him, and so—and so— —?"

"Shut up, Parsley. Don't you circulate it," put in his neighbour hastily. "Heaven send Lady Henrietta hasn't got hold of that."

"By George, if the tale came to her ears— —!"

The last man mended his pace. He had hung back a little.

"Rackham's bearing to the right," he struck in. "You can hear the horse trotting on the hill. He must be turning in to see Lady Henrietta. I wonder what on earth she wants him for. It was a rather portentous message."

They had reached a rougher bit of road and their voices grew indistinct, drowned in a tired clatter of horses' hoofs, and died away in the distance.

Rackham himself could not guess the reason for Lady Henrietta's summons. Latterly there had been war between him and his aunt. Something must have happened to mitigate the rigour of her ban, but he rather fancied the circumstances must be uncommon that could accomplish that. He was curious, and not the less so when, having left his horse to a bucket of gruel, he walked stiffly across from the stables, and letting himself in at the hall door, found himself face to face with another visitor, who had just arrived and was slipping off her furs.

"Julia!" he said, taken aback at her presence in this house. She acknowledged his amazement with a trickling laugh. Her voice had a note of melancholy importance.

"Is it so unnatural," she said reproachfully, "that you should find me here?"

The man bit his lip, looking at her. To him there was humour in her romantic pose.

CHAPTER II

They had once been so well acquainted—though lately she had affected short-sightedness when she saw him—that he imagined he understood her. He rather admired an invincible vanity that had ignored disappointment and defied scoffing tongues by making this bid for public sympathy. It was a brilliant move, but he had never thought it would impose on Lady Henrietta, that worldly woman with a hot corner in her heart for anybody who could squeeze in, but an implacable spirit. She had held out stubbornly up to now.

"Well—I don't know," he said, hesitating, swallowing his amusement.

Julia lifted her tragic eyes to his. Perhaps she was not sorry he should witness her recognition in this house. The trailing black garments that she was wearing for Barnaby lent a majestic sweep to her full outlines, and there was a kind of bloom on her cheeks. She reminded one of a big purple pansy.

The butler, an old family servant, one of those that know too much, had closed the great door, shutting out the wind and the stormy sky, already night-ridden; and was now waiting discreetly in the background. Rackham nodding to him, remarked a curious twinkle on his face, but when he looked again it was wooden.

"I knew she would send for me at last," crowed Julia. "People called her selfish and cruel, but I told everybody I understood. I told them to give her time. It must be so difficult for her to realise that someone else was closer to poor Barnaby than even she. How could she help feeling, at first, a little jealousy of my grief?"

"I was sent for, too," said Rackham bluntly. "She said she had something to show me."

"Poor dear!" said Julia. "How touching that she should think of it. You were his cousin, and she wants you to witness her do me justice."

The man smiled to himself at her manner of glancing backwards at their fellowship in disgrace. Was it possible that his aunt had really made up her mind to forget and forgive, and fall upon Julia's neck? He felt a twinge of something like shame.

"We mustn't keep her waiting," said Julia. "Is she in the library, Macdonald? That is where she used to sit...."

Already she was assuming her ancient intimacy with the ways of the house, and the servant made way for her as she passed him, traversing the hall with a mournful swagger.

Lady Henrietta was knitting hard.

She sat in a deep sofa by the fire, turned so that it faced the hangings that screened off the outer hall. The library was so big that it seemed to reach at either end into darkness, and the lamps made little islands of brilliance here and there in the prevailing gloom. Behind, with the books, there was another fireplace, a red and glimmering hearth where two or three dogs lay, warm and sleepy, dreaming of winter tramps and a man calling them to heel. One, a terrier with a bitten ear, had started half-awake on a run down the room, but she could not settle on the other rug, and came back restlessly to her post on the shabbier tiger-skin.

Barnaby's mother had a thin, hard, eager face, with a flick of colour high on her cheek-bones. Not an unkind woman, but one possessed by some passion that had tempered a frivolous, careless nature to a mood of iron. Her rings glittered as she knitted, and the wires clicked faster and faster, as if it were impossible that her fingers could be for a minute still. She was knitting a man's grey-green shooting stocking.

Occasionally her eyes, with a strange spark in them, lit on a girl sitting opposite, gazing into the fire. The girl was young and quiet; her head shone dark in the ring of light; her cheek was pale, but her short upper lip showed courage. Lady Henrietta watched her with a fierce joy that was not yet liking.

"You're not at all what I expected," she said abruptly. "I was afraid of what I would see, and I didn't dare to look at you when you arrived last night;—but twenty times I turned the handle of your bedroom door. At last, I poked my head in when you were asleep, just to know the worst.—I nearly dropped the candle when I saw your little head on the pillow."

"What did you expect?" the girl said faintly.

"A great, coarse, fine woman, snoring," said Lady Henrietta.

All at once she bent forward, putting her knitting into the girl's hands. There was significance in the gesture.

"Pick up that stitch for me," she said. "He never liked ladders in his stockings."

There was no shake in the hard jauntiness of her voice, but the girl, searching with bent head for the dropped stitch, felt her fingers tremble as they touched the rough worsted—felt something pluck at her heart. Barnaby was dead, and she had never known him; but he was the one real person walking through a dream in which she had lost herself.

She was not strong yet. She still had a trick of putting out her hand to some steady object when she stood up alone. And at first she had not understood—too ill to question, not wondering. It was as if she had died one night and awakened to a consciousness of protection, a mystery of care and kindness, of strangers who took charge of her, treating her like a precious doll. When she at last knew the reason, she had felt like one who, falling from a precipice, found herself clinging, the dizzy horror stopped by a branch;—she could not let it go.

So they had found her, and brought her over the sea, and put her to bed in a great, comfortable room, in a house that was haunted. It was Barnaby's house, and it was for Barnaby's sake that people were kind to her. Somehow they were all shadows to her beside the thought of him. His name had been invoked to shelter her; it had been enough to lift her out of despair. She had begun to feel safe in a confused assurance that she belonged to him.

She remembered last night. She remembered the door sliding softly, and a rustle in the room, and how she had lain quite still, shutting her eyes, holding her breath, startled out of sleep. Someone was smoothing the bedclothes under her chin. She longed to cover her face, but could not. It was not a ghost, for mortal fingers had touched her cheek. Soon the rustle had withdrawn from her bedside, and she had heard a little sound that might have been a sigh. Afterwards the door had closed, and the room was empty.

Seized by an unaccountable impulse, she had put her foot to the floor, and crossed the wide carpet to the fireplace, where the visitor had gone from her side. The fire had fallen in, flaring high in a quivering blaze, and by its light she had seen that over the chimney-piece hung the picture of a man. Instinct had told her who it was, and she stared at him, fascinated.

The other woman had left her the wrong photograph in her hurry. This was no weak boy with a foolish mouth, bundled over-seas by his people. This was a man with a steady face that betrayed nothing of himself, and eyes that held her startled gaze. Blue eyes, audacious and understanding. Her heart beat strangely. For this must be Barnaby the reckless, who had married a wife and got himself killed ... and she, poor fool, was calling herself his widow.

She clung to the chimney-piece, shivering with excitement, a quaint, slight figure in her white night-dress.

"I'll hurt nobody.... I'll hurt nobody!" she was explaining to him in an imploring whisper; and it seemed to her that the man in the picture smiled.

"—There, give it back to me," said Lady Henrietta jealously, and her voice scattered mists of imagination. "You don't think I'm crazy, do you? You know why it is I can't stop knitting his stockings.—We'll not talk about him, Susan. You and I have each our own memories, and we can't share them.—I don't want yours. But we'll fight for him together; since he belongs to us."

Her manner took on a sudden fierceness.

"I've not told anybody about you yet," she said. "I've been hugging the secret for purposes of my own. I am a wicked woman, Susan. Upon my honour, if you hadn't existed, I'd have been obliged to invent you. If you hadn't come to me, I'd have searched the world for an imitation, from end to end. How he would laugh at me!—But we'll not talk about him—we couldn't bear it. Only we'll fight for him, as I said. We'll not let his enemies triumph and pretend that they broke his heart."

Her voice was quicker, charged with a passionate haste that hurried the words out before she could close her lips.

"You little pale thing," she said. "I am not a kissing woman ... but ... oh, you don't know what you are to me. Wait. I'll make you understand. There's a creature here who behaved shamefully to my boy ... to *him*. And now he is dead she goes about boasting, claiming him as her victim, hinting to all who will listen that he killed himself for love of her. It's not true.... You'll teach them it is not true!"

She stopped, controlling herself. In the hall outside there was the slight bustle of an arrival, and voices, muffled by distance, came faintly through. As suddenly as she had spoken, she checked her outburst of confidence, and picked up her knitting with a terrible little smile.

"I know who it is that's coming," she said grimly. "A woman, Susan—a woman who dresses in black, and prates of a misunderstanding."

They came in together, the man blinking a little after his ride in the twilight, approaching with a stiff gait and clinking spurs; the woman swimming triumphantly up the room.

"Dear Lady Henrietta!" she murmured, a ready quiver in her emotional Irish voice.

"How do you do, Julia?" said Lady Henrietta. She had recovered an extraordinary calm. "Did you and Rackham meet on the doorstep? I am pleased to see you both."

Her ominous quietness struck the man, more observant. His instinct had not disappointed him, that was clear; he marked her attitude with an inward chuckle. Something tremendous was toward.

"You are looking well, Aunt Henrietta," he said politely. "Do you mind my smoking? We had a tiring day, and I missed my only sandwich."

"Macdonald will look after you," she said. "Make him get you anything you want."

"Thanks," said Rackham. "I'll have something before I go. I meant to ask him for a whisky and soda, but he shot us in here.—I thought the old chap seemed a bit excited."

"Yes," said Lady Henrietta. "They were all so devoted to Barnaby. Naturally they share my feelings—" She paused significantly, and he could see that she was watching Julia. "My son has given me a legacy.... He has left me his wife."

"How sweet of you to put it like that!" said Julia.

She had established herself on the sofa without an instant's delay, taking figurative possession, too self-absorbed to appreciate any by-play. Her head was full of the tardy capitulation of her fellow-mourner, and she, in her own eyes, was the principal figure here. But Rackham, looking on, all but shouted.

"What?" he said. "Poor old Barnaby! Married? Good Lord! how did it come about?"

Julia turned round and stared at him.

"Lord Rackham!" she said. "Are you mad?"

Lady Henrietta made a motion with her hand towards the girl sitting in the background. She could not trust herself to speak to the woman whose outrageous complacency had survived her blow.

"My dear," she said, "this is your husband's cousin. He gets everything when I die—things are so wickedly entailed in this family—except a pittance I mean to scrape up for you. You know I don't chatter, Rackham. You can understand I didn't care to set the neighbourhood talking until I had Susan here."

There was no mistaking the triumphant note in her proclamation.

The girl coloured faintly. They were all looking at her now; the strange woman with a startled face, the man curiously. Some likeness in him to the picture that hung upstairs troubled her. So Barnaby might have looked, his dare-devil glance falling on her with a quizzical compassion.

Rackham's wits were not slow. He crossed over to her side, and took up his station on the hearthrug, so close to her that his splashed scarlet coat almost brushed her black sleeve. Barnaby had been dressed like him in the picture, gallant in hunting clothes. Would Barnaby have stood by her? For she understood the significance of his action. This man wanted to be her friend. She trembled a little, wondering why.

Lady Henrietta took no more notice of him than if he had been a vexing shadow put in his place. His strategic movement was lost on her. Barnaby's mother, in her thirst to punish, her eagerness in striking for the sake of her son, had not time to consider that the sword in her hand was his wife. Her eyes were shining with the fire that had burnt up her tears, and they were fixed on the enchantress who had wrecked Barnaby's life, and was trading on his old infatuation, making a bid for public sympathy by flaunting her forfeited hold on him.

"I can't understand," said Julia, with a gasp. "Barnaby was not married...."

But she was shaken. Her blank amazement was turning visibly to dismay. This stroke was so sharp, so inconceivable, that she lost her head, refusing to believe in the humbling revelation.

"It's a plot!" she cried all at once. "A plot against me. What have I done to be treated like this? Why should I be insulted?—Everybody knows that Barnaby and I——"

"Don't be an idiot, Julia," said Rackham softly, but it was not his interruption that stopped her passionate surrender to the Irish-woman's instinct to have it out with the world.

Perhaps the actress was uppermost in Susan, or perhaps an odd impulse of loyalty to the dead man whose ring she wore carried her out of herself. Her heart was hot against the woman who had played fast and loose with him, and it taught her how one who belonged to Barnaby would have faced this moment. His wife would not be a coward, would not sit, a piteous listener, in the background; she had his memory to uphold. And so she found herself standing up, confronting the stranger in a proud silence that was more eloquent than reproach. Slowly, without a word, she moved onwards to leave the room.

"Gad!" said Rackham, under his breath. He liked that.

Something like awe had smitten Julia. She remained a moment transfixed, staring after her, all exclamation hushed on her reckless lips. Then, all at once, she followed.

"Tell me who you are," she panted hysterically. "It's all nonsense, isn't it?— It's a sham?"

Lady Henrietta was watching the scene from her sofa, and so was Rackham, standing with his back to the fire. They were both far off. It was a swift and dramatic minute.

"His mother hates me," said Julia, half to herself; her hold tightened on the girl's arm. "She's capable of anything. She—What colour were his eyes?"

The question was flung at her without warning. But a man's face stood out distinct in the girl's imagination, haunting her with a clearness none of these other faces had; smiling whimsically down from his picture all this while she was letting people proclaim her his.... Somehow she was defending him, covering his hurt.

Without thinking, without a pause—

"Blue," she said.

The other woman's hand dropped. She let her go.

Susan let the velvet hangings fall heavily behind her as she came through. A kind of wonder at herself possessed her, and her knees trembled. Mechanically she traversed the hall, and began to climb the wide staircase, leaning a little as she went, on the solid oak balustrade.

On the first landing a window faced the stair, and right and left ran corridors, interminable, and equally mysterious to the stranger, who was, in a manner, lost in this unknown house. She sank down on the window-seat, set deep in the thickness of the wall.

Outside, the sky was dark with a strange red, as of furnaces under the horizon, glimmering in the west. She could just distinguish the jutting corner of the more antique part of the house, built as it was in different centuries, bit by bit. That side was strangely ornamented with mediæval figures—the images of ancient warriors, all battered and weather-stained. And the land they had won was quiet, lying half asleep; only the trees still restless as night came on.

She turned her face. In front of her gleamed the shallow stair, running straight into the hall below, and all the way down hung pictures, men and women who had lived in this house, and trod the stairs, hurrying, lagging, or perhaps clinging, as she had in her weakness clung to the balustrade. Some were ill-painted, some stared wickedly; but all of them were watching. There was history in their eyes.

The girl felt a queer fellowship with the still procession; she, whose only title among them was make-believe. Perhaps, in forgotten times, her own people had fought and loved and ridden side by side with these, and their descendant had come back to a friend's house. How good it would be to let the world go on, to walk in a dream always, and not struggle any more.

She thought, with a remote disdain, of the scene downstairs. Her heart was still beating quickly; but that gripping sense of the theatre had left her. And she knew she had conquered. Barnaby's memory was safe from the woman his mother hated. One could imagine her claim collapsing, one could hear her voluble excuse, pleading bewilderment, accepting the situation—with perhaps a plaintive expression of her relief in knowing she was, after all, not as guilty as gossip said—had Lady Henrietta heard the dreadful rumours? And Barnaby's mother would smile at the thrust with victory in her soul, while the man, his cousin, would look on, smothering his chuckle, with his head on one side like a magpie, and a splash of mud that had dried on his cheek.

It was his step she heard first as they came out into the hall. He and Julia were leaving together, she talking fast. Her voice, charged with subdued excitement, rose and fell on a singing note. What she was saying did not reach up the stairs; only its contralto music. The sound of it awakened Susan in her mood of overwrought exaltation. Reality came back to her with a shock. She remembered another voice as warm, as emotional, with the same theatrical tune of tears; and she remembered the dangerous charity that had mocked her opposition. Stripped of its fantastic mist of adventure, she looked at her own story, and was ashamed. Her very scorn of the woman against whom she had been pitted turned on herself and scorched her, ranking her as low. She and Julia—no, she could not bear to be judged with Julia. The romantic sophistry that had comforted her was gone, and nothing could stay her desperate longing to be honest.

They passed underneath. Rackham was helping Julia into her furs, was hunting for her muff, with his face to the stair. The girl above held her breath. His nearness affected her with a kind of panic.

She had an intuition that he was the kind of man who would—guess. She thought of his quick movement to her side, his presumptuous readiness to stand by her, unspoken but unmistakable, with an unexplained alarm. Would they never go? Why did he loiter, looking upwards with that inexplicable smile?

As the great door shut, at last, on a silence, she sprang up and went downstairs. It was a pity she was not stronger. One should not go to be judged with a tottering step. And she would want all her courage. Knowing the spirit in which Barnaby's mother had dealt with Julia, she did not look for mercy.

But Lady Henrietta was not sitting upright and watchful, with that look of ruthlessness stamped on her thin, hard, pretty face. She had thrown herself across the sofa, her fast-knitting fingers idle, the half-finished stocking that would never be worn fallen from her hand to the floor. She lay like a broken reed; deprived of the motive that had sustained her—and she was crying.

That sight stirred all the heart in Susan. She ran to her blindly, only conscious of a great compassion that shamed her selfish terror of the weight of a lie. She could not tell her ... now.

And Barnaby's mother looked up at her approach. Something of the old defiant jauntiness came back to her for a minute. She tried to laugh.

"Come here and kiss me," she called. There was a fierce tenderness in her cry—"you darling—!"

CHAPTER III

Susan had flung from her with both hands the imprudent longing to cry out her story.

Somehow she felt that if she spoke now she would be a traitor. It was too late to look back; for good or ill she had changed places with the other woman who would not come. To fail now would not be to clear her honour, it would be to desert her post.

When Lady Henrietta, having triumphed, had given way at last, and had clung to Susan, the girl, gathered in that fierce clasp, had known that Barnaby's mother took passionate comfort in her only because the stranger was something that had belonged to him. To deny her that comfort would be to rob one who had nothing left. Could she, by a wistful life of devotion, justify herself, not in the sight of man, not to hard judges—but perhaps to this Barnaby who was dead, and who would surely understand? Keeping silent, she promised him that she would.

Day after day passed over her head, building an unsteady wall between her and that pitiless outside world in which she had been like a driven leaf, without hope or foothold. She became accustomed to the lazy peace of the house, to the watchful offices of the old servants, who seemed, like Lady Henrietta herself, curiously proud of her.

Slowly she grew stronger; her thin cheek rounded, still pale, but touched with a faint promise of colour.

One afternoon she was taking her solitary walk in the park, and had wandered farther than she had been. The dogs had left her, scurrying after rabbits, and she leaned on a stile that offered a resting-place, a little tired and wistful, gazing at the sinking fire in the west.

Suddenly the air was quick with galloping, and all around her were jumping horses. Startled, but unafraid, she watched them coming over the hedge, imagining that as they came they would vanish.

"You shouldn't stay there, you might get hurt," called someone, pulling up at her side. "How are you?"

She had been looking on, as one would look at a gallant picture, not realizing that she was in its midst. Instinctively she drew back. All had stopped, and hounds were clustering in the bottom, where the huntsman had dismounted, and was peering into a drain. Many heads were turned, with a rough kindness that excused curiosity, in her direction. Perhaps they were all Barnaby's comrades, who missed him, and saw in the pathetic figure one who was missing him more than they...

CHAPTER III

But the man who had drawn up beside her was leaning down to her like an old friend, barring out the rest with his shoulder. His horse, still excited, jerked at his bit, and flung a white flick of lather on her black dress. Without thinking, she stretched out her hand to his muzzle.

"Take care. He's an uncertain brute," said Rackham. "You like horses?"

"I used to ride," she said.

Something awoke in her at that velvet touch, and she could not finish, thinking of other horses.

"Good," he said quickly. "Tell you what. I have a mare that would carry you. I'll come and talk it over—if my aunt will let me in."

He laughed a little under his breath at that. "How do you get on with her?" he asked. "*She's* a warrior—!"

Susan lifted her eyes to his face. His abrupt friendliness could not entirely conquer the fluttering apprehension of danger in his good-nature that made her unaccountably shy of him. There was commiseration in his look—and admiration.

"Look here," he said; "we're cousins—by marriage. I've some warrant to be officious—and you're alone in a strange land, aren't you?—and all that."

Was it her imagination, or did he drop his voice significantly? Perhaps he was glancing at their first meeting, pitying her as a reed bruised in Lady Henrietta's warlike hands. Perhaps—no, she could not read his expression.

The huntsman straightened his back, and walked stiffly towards his horse. A man who was giving up passed by and gravely took off his hat; she watched him hooking with his whip at the bridle gate. She was afraid that they would all ride off and leave her with Barnaby's kinsman, and his penetrating smile.

"Anyhow," said Rackham, "I'm here if you want backing.... Just let me know if you need any kind of help."

A scream on the hidden side of the spinney beneath them linked up the field, believing in one of the glorious surprises that light up the dragging end of the day. The huntsman pushed right through the misty tangle, calling on his hounds, and the riders disappeared like a swirling river. A minute and they were gone.

The girl listened breathlessly to the thudding of distant hoofs. Her heart beat a little too fast, disturbed by that brief interlude of excitement. She stood quite still until the last gleam of scarlet faded, and the galloping died away, leaving a tremendous quiet. There was no sound at last but the wildfowl, far away on the lake, beginning their sunset chaunt.

Half the household had rushed out to look for hounds, and were returning singly, more or less out of breath, as the girl came home. It was astonishing what a commotion the hunt, in its passing, had awakened in that sad household. Lady Henrietta herself, with a shawl on her head, was in the garden, peering. Her sporting instincts were struggling in her with a kind of rage.

"Tell me who were out," she said. "Oh, of course you can't. But *they* would know who you are. I am glad they saw you. It would remind some of them—a man is so soon forgotten! To think of them all hunting and fooling just as they used; with him left out—! Did they run from Tilton? I don't suppose a man of them wasted a thought on him till they saw you there. Did they change foxes, Susan?"

She talked on eagerly, answering herself with conjecture as she hurried the girl into the warm house, out of the gathering rain. Macdonald, the butler, was better informed than she, and his mistress seized on him as he slipped in, wiping his brow, short-winded but triumphant. He it was who had holloaed the fox away.

"Come here and tell me all about it," said Lady Henrietta sharply. "—At your age, Macdonald—!"

He approached with solemnity, remembering his dignity, and his rheumatism, an inextinguishable light in his eye.

"They ran from Owston, my lady, and lost the fox on yon side of our bottom spinney. He must have been about done, by the way scent failed, and they couldn't pick him up again for the gentlemen crowding forrard. No, my lady, there was two sticks crossed in the earth—and the drainpipe clogged. But we found 'em one that'll take them a sight farther than some of them care to go. A real fine fox that was!" He wound up with real pride.

"And who was that on the bay?" asked Lady Henrietta. "He took the fence well, Macdonald."

"That was his Lordship," allowed Macdonald, but grudgingly. "Ah, my lady, I seen Mr. Barnaby take that very jump that day they killed their fox in the park. Clean and fine he went up, and lighted; he never smashed no top rail!"

"I know—I know," said Lady Henrietta. "The day he put out his shoulder."

"That was a rabbit hole," said Macdonald jealously. "Ah, my lady, his Lordship will never go like him!"

Dismissing Rackham with the scorn of an old servant staunch to his master, he shook his head mournfully and retreated. Lady Henrietta had turned abruptly from her cross-examination, and held out her hands to the fire.

The incident, slight as it was, and brief, coloured all their evening. Afterwards, Lady Henrietta returned to the subject, amusing herself with surmises. Had Susan noticed a man with a grizzled moustache and a furtive eye?—and another who had a trick of jerking out his elbow?—and one who rode like a jack-in-the-box, starting up continually in his stirrups? And had she seen a woman in brown, who usually backed in under the hedge at a check, talking secrets with a lank man, her shadow,—and all unwitting that there were two sides to hedges, and that voices filtered through? Insensibly, she branched into reminiscence, telling caustic histories of these Leicestershire unworthies, who were all unknown to Susan; and the girl hardly listened, sitting with her cheek on her hand and a dreaming brow.

The short interlude had impressed her. But in imagination she saw, not the splendid figure that had crashed over the hedge down yonder,—but another, one silently haunting the dim pastures where he had ridden once, sweeping out of the

CHAPTER III

dusk, and passing into the dusk again. The swift scene came back to her, with its wild rush of life, hounds, and horsemen, — only, instead of his cousin, she pictured Barnaby, to whose memory she had dedicated herself.

It was wearing late. Soon Lady Henrietta would interrupt herself, breaking off with a remorseful brusqueness, and order her off to bed. How quiet it was in the library, that vast, comfortable room! How safe she felt, and how sleepy, only dreaming, not thinking of anything.

The white fox-terrier with the bitten ear had stolen down to her and lay on her skirt. There was a kind of fellowship between her and the dog. When it jumped up all at once with a shiver she stroked its back softly, wondering why it alone was excited by the wind whistling outside the house. And it looked up in her face and scuttled like a thing possessed down the room.

"What's the matter with Kit?" said Lady Henrietta, pausing. — "I daresay she heard Macdonald shutting up in the hall." — And she went on talking.

Far down the room the heavy curtain swung hastily, and fell back. It was Susan who, without warning, lifted her eyes and saw somebody standing there.

He had walked right in out of the wind and rain, had flung off his dripping cap, but had not waited to unbutton his greatcoat; and he looked as he had looked in his picture, but no ghost — real, — with dreadful blue eyes, and a smiling mouth.

The girl started to her feet. One wild moment she stared at him. Her own cry sounded strange in her ears, very far off ... and then the world went round.

*****

Slowly she drifted back into consciousness, and she was lying on her bed, surrounded by fluttered women, whose amazed whispering reached her like the dim clamour in a dream.

"Poor thing; poor thing — it was too much for her." "It was wicked of Mr. Barnaby to startle her like that. But how like him — —!"

"Lord, Lord! his face as she lay on the floor! — and his mother rating him as if he'd never been dead an hour — —!"

"'You've killed her!' said she. 'You've killed her!'"

"Like as not she'll go out of her mind, poor lamb!"

The quavering excitement hushed suddenly as she stirred.

"Hold your noise, you!" the old housekeeper adjured the others, pushing them on one side, and patting her anxiously, promising something in a voice that shook, tremulous and coaxing, — as one might dangle the moon to quiet a frantic child.

Up the long corridor came a man's step, and the pattering of a dog. The housekeeper jumped, and ran from the bedside, and the maids clung hysterically together, looking with a scared eagerness at the door. A superstitious terror was still painted on their faces.

Barnaby was not dead. The whole dreadful comedy was scarcely clear to the girl, so dizzy was she with this one miracle, the thing that was impossible, and was true. Shame had not yet burnt up wonder. She lay motionless, with her hands on her heart, listening to his step, and waiting for the sound of a voice that she had never heard.

"How is she?"

Oh strange, kind voice, asking that! Susan caught her breath, remembering who she was not.

The housekeeper, running out, had closed the door nervously, and was posted with her back against it, half in a rapture, and half reproachful.

"Oh, Mr. Barnaby—! Oh, my gracious!"

Collecting herself, she went on in a trembling hurry.

"She's come round at last; she's come to herself;—but the doctor says we must keep her quiet. You can't come in, sir! It might do harm. He said so before he went to my lady.... I daren't let you in, Mr. Barnaby.... Please! ... I've told her you'll come to her in the morning ... and I was to give you her love."

The girl started up, horror-stricken, and fell back on the bed, covering her face. Would nothing silence that foolish tongue, inspired by its ill-judged haste to pacify the presumed impatience of the man who had done the mischief? Through the guarded door, through her shut eyes, Susan had a scorching vision of Barnaby, the stranger, listening to that brazen message. And between her convulsive fingers she heard the old servant babbling on.... No, after that, she could not bear to look him in the face!

Panic seized her. It grew upon her as she lay quiescent, enduring the ministrations of sympathizers who would have scorned to touch her if they had known. Barnaby had not spoken. He had not said to them, "She is an impostor." He was letting them pity her, handle her gently ... till to-morrow.

They had given her something to make her sleep, but the draught was impotent; instead of soothing, it was exciting a strange confusion in her head. She got out of bed at last, hearing nothing but somewhere in her room the heavy breathing of a dozing watcher. Slowly at first, and then quicker, as the impulse took hold of her, she began struggling into her clothes. She must go, she must go; she could not stay in this house.

Driven by her panic, that could not think, could not reason, she set her desperate foot on the stair.

The lights were not out in the hall below; they shimmered faintly as she passed like a shadow towards the door. If someone should come—! Feverishly she tried to undo the bar; the latch was very heavy. Her heart beat so loud that she was deaf to all other noises.

She did not know that she was not alone till a hand was laid on her shoulder.

She turned round, shaking from head to foot, leaning against the door.

"Oh, let me go!" she cried.

CHAPTER III

He looked at her gravely.

"I'm afraid we're neither of us real," he said. "Let's try not to scare each other.... They tell me that you're my widow."

She turned her face from him.

"Don't look at me. Oh, don't look at me! Let me go," she repeated wildly.

His fingers closed over hers, still fumbling at the bar.

"I don't think I can do that," he said. "The doctor blames me for frightening you out of your life. He'd hold me responsible if I let you rush out of my house in the middle of the night like this. If you don't mind I'll ask you not to make me out a worse fool than I've been already. And—you aren't going to faint again, are you? Sit down a minute——"

His arm went round her quickly; he had unloosed her hands from the door, and put her into a chair by the fire, before she was sure that she had not fainted. She leant her whirling head against the packed red cushions.

"They gave me something to make me sleep...." she murmured.

He stood a little way off on the hearthrug, watching her. Kit, the terrier, lay down suddenly between them, as if it had him safe.

"How did you know me?" he said abruptly.

"There is a picture of you," she said; "and I—thought of you so often."

The man who had been dismissed so lightly from his world looked down with a queer expression. He could not doubt the utter unconsciousness in the tired young voice. She had nothing to hope for. She was being judged.

"In the name of Heaven, why——?" he burst out, checking himself too late for, the girl stood up and faced him, calling up all her courage.

"Because I am a shameless wretch," she cried unsteadily. "A liar and an impostor.... You don't ask a thief why he has robbed you. You send him to prison.... You don't laugh at him...."

"You child!" said Barnaby.

The strange, kind note in his voice broke down her desperation. Somehow, she found herself stammering out the story of her Southern childhood; the brave old family ruined by the war; the last of them dying, the last friend gone, and she left undefended, to fight for herself in the world. Not strong enough to nurse the sick, not hard enough to win her way in business; driven to try if she could live by her one poor gift of acting;—what could she do but catch at the happy-go-lucky kindness that had flung salvation to her?

"I could have died..." she said, scorning herself; "but I ... came."

"Hush!" said the man softly, all at once, turning round to meet interruption. The doctor was coming downstairs, deliberately, as became an all-wise and elderly dictator, peering short-sightedly into the hall below.

"Bless my soul!" he said. "Barnaby, you villain, she's not fit to be talking to you. I warned the servants it was as much as their lives were worth to let you go near her;—and look at this!"

He shook his head at them both, but relented, with his fingers on Susan's pulse. His professional knowledge of woman mitigated his surprise at her quick recovery. Some women could bear anything, after the first shock of pain or joy.

"Good," he said. "Since you're awake, and in your right mind, which I had hardly dared to hope for,—I'll send you up to Lady Henrietta. She has been calling for you. Just sit beside her, and tell her very quietly, over and over again, how Barnaby looks, and all that. I can't risk her seeing him yet;—her age isn't so elastic,—and nothing will satisfy her but you."

Instinctively the girl moved to obey, and stopped. Would Barnaby let her go to his mother? As far as she could understand—it was still stranger than a dream—he had not yet proclaimed her an impostor. But surely the time was come.

"Oh," said the doctor, following her look; "your husband must do without you."

And then Barnaby spoke.

"You're a bit hard on us, doctor," he said. "We had a lot to say to each other. But my wife and I can finish our talk to-morrow."—His voice, as he turned to her, lost its humorous note and became grave. "Go up to my mother,—please."

She went. The doctor watched her go, and, shaking off a certain perplexity, addressed himself to the younger man. Old friend of the family that he was, his gruff manner poorly hid his emotion.

"Good heavens, man!" he said. "I can't get accustomed to you. Shake hands again, will you? I want to feel positive you are not a spook."

"What about my mother?" asked Barnaby. He too had been watching the girl go slowly up the stairs.

"She'll be all right, if we can keep her quiet," said the doctor cheerfully. "But she can't afford to have any more shocks. Her heart is bad. You didn't know that, of course. She is a courageous lady, and has taken all your vagaries gallantly up to now, but this has been a bit too sudden. If it hadn't been for your wife's collapse distracting her attention for the moment, taking her mind off the greater shock——"

He broke off there.

"How the devil was I to know?" burst out the other man. "I had no notion that I was dead."

"Hadn't you heard——?"

"How should I? Look here, doctor, I haven't been sulking in civilization; racketing in cities. I've been roughing it, going up and down in the earth.—There wasn't much use in writing letters. I told my mother I would turn up again some day, and she wasn't to be surprised. I did send her a line, now and then, the last of them a greasy scrawl in a mining camp, where there was one bit of paper among

CHAPTER III

the lot of us, and I won it. She can't have got that.... When I had worked the restlessness out of my blood—some fellows can't manage that, it takes them all their lives—I had a fancy to come home and walk into the old place as if I had never left it.... It's simple enough——!"

He was bending forward, stammering a little in his excitement. Suddenly he laughed.

"By George!" he said. "So that was why the porters fled from me at John o' Gaunt!"

The old man surveyed him anxiously, wiping his glasses.

Often one heard of men who, seized by a thirst for adventure in the rough, or unbalanced by passion and disappointment, had thrown up everything familiar and dropped out, to savour the hard realities of life. Sometimes they reappeared, sometimes only peculiar stories drifted to their old set about them, and those who might know were dumb. He felt a most irrational alarm, an impulse to hold fast to this prodigal.

"You'll not vanish again?" he said hastily. "You won't want to roam in search of adventures now you have a wife to take care of."

Barnaby stretched out for a cigarette and lit it. There had always been a box of them in one corner of the chimney-piece. It did not strike him as odd that he should find them there.

"Have a smoke, doctor," he said. "It'll steady your nerves a bit.... Yes, I'm sobered."

He halted a minute, and the terrier at his feet, remembering an old trick he had taught her, sprang up and blew out the match. As he stooped to caress her, she began licking him furiously. There had been some other trick, but she had forgotten that. She made a clumsy effort to keep his attention by crossing her paws and waving them, which was how it had begun....

"Good dog," he said, and she dropped at his feet, proud of her cleverness, though grudging his notice to the doctor.

"You're right there," he went on, as if the thought amused him. "A man is a fool to go tramping over the world, searching for adventures, when they come to him on his own hearth."

*****

Lady Henrietta lay propped high with pillows, talking fast.

"I want Susan!" she complained. "Bring me Susan. The doctor shan't put me off with his opiates. I can't trust any of you but Susan."

And the girl came faltering into the room.

Lady Henrietta caught her hand, nipping it tight in hers.

"Susan, my child," she said. "What a little cold hand you've got! They're hushing me as if I was a lunatic, humouring me with tales. And my heart's so funny. I can feel it misbehaving.... I'll die if they make me angry. Come here, closer. I want to ask you—*you* won't tell me comfortable lies.—Has Barnaby come back?"

"He has come back," said Susan.

"Are you deceiving me?" whispered Lady Henrietta. "Are you in league with the doctor?—I sent old Dawson out there, you know, and he said the report was true.... He saw the boy's grave. He put up a stone.... And the lawyers came croaking together like ravens, and swore there wasn't a scrap of doubt.... And Rackham stepped into his shoes, and I made them search for you high and low!—Oh! no, it's not true! I am wandering in my mind. Look at me. You and I couldn't cheat each other. Let me see it in your face!"

But Susan could not. She dropped her head over the hand clasping hers so fiercely, and her unstrung nerves gave way; she could not keep from sobbing.

Strangely enough, her crying seemed to soothe Lady Henrietta.

"Ah, you never used to cry like that!" she said. "He has come." She stroked the girl's hair with her other hand.

"I suppose they'll let me see him in the morning," she said rationally. "He will be asleep now, poor boy. He shall come up to me when he has had his breakfast, and pour out his ridiculous adventures. They must give him devilled bacon. Margaret, Margaret, stop snivelling, and remind them to give him devilled bacon. Keep holding my hand, Susan, and don't cry so. We have got him back."

CHAPTER IV

The dim light was already struggling in through the curtains before Lady Henrietta dropped off to sleep, quieted. Susan dared not withdraw her hand. Her arm grew stiff, ached awhile, and was numb; her head slid against the pillow, and her eyes shut at last.

She awakened with a start to hear Lady Henrietta's laugh, weak but natural, and a man's exclamation, sharp and pitiful, above her.

"Take her away, Barnaby, and give her her breakfast," his mother was ordering. "Didn't you see her? The poor child has been sitting up holding my hand like that the livelong night. I was clean off my head.... I might have known you'd behave like this. Oh, I can bear the sight of you now; don't be nervous; I'm not one of those sentimental mothers—! But since I've taken to heart attacks I have to be treated with circumspection"—she desisted a minute in her rapid effort to disguise emotion:—"Barnaby, I am obliged to you for—for *her*."

"You're fond of her, are you, mother?" said Barnaby.

Lady Henrietta laughed at him, amused at his queer intonation.

"Fond?" she cried. "I adore her. The first minute I saw her, a little pale wisp in her widow's weeds, I adored her. She isn't your style at all, you puzzle. You used to admire a more lavish figure.... I can't understand it in the least; but I'm thankful. And that reminds me you must take her up to London immediately, and have her put into proper clothes."

"Oh, I say——" Barnaby was beginning. She took the words out of his mouth.

"Yes, it's your business," she said. "We can't have her going about in black; it denies your existence—! and you look like a battered scamp yourself. You'll have to go to your tailor. If you want any money I'll write you a cheque.... They won't honour yours while you're dead.... Wake her up now, and take her away to breakfast—and take care of her if you can!"

He bent down and touched her arm, and she lifted her head, still dazed, and stood up from her cramped position.

"Run away," said Lady Henrietta. "Run away, you two. I am going to wash my face."

She kissed her hand to them as they went through the door, and, in spite of herself, her lip quivered. She lay quite still for a minute, raging at herself.

"Quiet!" she muttered. "Quiet! It's nothing to die about, stupid heart!"

Downstairs the servants were all hovering, lying in wait, and watching for a glimpse of the master. Macdonald himself had drawn two arm-chairs beside a small table by the fire, and unwillingly, but discreetly, took himself off and closed the door behind him.

"Sit down," said Barnaby gently. "I'll pour out your tea. You must want it."

She let him do as he would, accepting her cup at his hands, drinking obediently, trying to eat; patient, but not at all understanding him. The winter sun streamed in red, shining in her hair, making lights in its curling darkness; it even lent a fictitious pink to her cheek as she sat, so soberly, facing the man in whose house she was, whose ring was on her finger. When she turned her head a little the glimmer died. Irrelevantly—why should the thing strike him then?—he likened her paleness to the creamy tint of the hawthorn blossom, warm, and smoother than the wintry white of the sloe. She had been ill, too; she was very fragile.

All the while she dared hardly glance at him, though she knew that he was regarding her, not with the righteous wrath of a swindled Briton whose house was his castle, but with a strange expression that, less comprehensible, was little less alarming. The situation seemed to amuse him.... And it was like a scene in a play; intimate, domestic, and yet unreal. They were obliged to sit so close at the confidential little table, with its clinking china, and its neighbouring row of silver dishes keeping warm in the fender.... She had a wild fancy that if she thrust her hand in that fire that leapt and crackled so naturally it would not burn.

"Well," he said suddenly. "What's to be done?"

He had risen and come round to her side; the little delay was over. They had finished breakfast....

"I don't know," she said. "I am at your mercy."

"Do you mind if I smoke?"

His matter-of-fact politeness, as he waited with the cigarette unlit between his fingers, provoked in her a fugitive smile.

"There!" he said. "You are beginning to see the funny side of it too, as I do. A man who has knocked about the world as I have doesn't bluster like a Pharisee and a brute, unless he is mad,—or angry. What on earth could I do to you?"

"Are you not—angry?" she asked faintly.

"Not exactly," said Barnaby. "I am rather astonished at your pluck. Of course, it was frightfully dangerous, and you have got us both into a hole.—I'm not going to preach at you——"

He hesitated a little.

"You know," he said. "I'm an awfully prudent chap, but once or twice in my life I have lost my head. When I went to America three years ago, I was only fit to be clapped into a strait-waistcoat. Of course, I did the first mad thing that came into my head."

There was a touch of some old bitterness in his voice then, and a sort of retro-

CHAPTER IV

spective contempt.

"It's a grim fact, that," he said. "It can't be got over. I don't know what possessed me;—but there *was* a marriage."

"She is very beautiful," said Susan, uttering her own wandering thought. She did not know why.

"Who?" said Barnaby. "Oh,—yes. She was like somebody I knew."

There was silence between them. Then the man laughed.

"It was one of those unaccountable acts of temporary madness," he said. "We're all guilty of such at times. Did she tell you why we fell out? How she mistook me for a sort of prince in disguise, and turned on me afterwards, as furious as I was—disillusioned? Don't let's talk about that. We have our own problem to consider."

"Yes," said the girl, catching her breath.

"I am afraid," he said gravely, "we must keep it up for a bit."

"I—don't—understand," she said.

"It's the only thing to do," he said. "Look at it fairly. Since the lady who married me sent you over as her substitute, she can't complain if I should acknowledge you as my wife. It injures nobody.—Don't mistake me!"

For the girl had sprung to her feet, and was gazing at him with horror in her eyes.

"Wait!" he said. "I'm not one of these talking fellows.—Perhaps I'm not putting it clearly. As far as I can make out, the doctor believes another shock on the top of this one might possibly kill my mother. She's not to be worried or contradicted. I can't go to her and tell her, 'That girl you are so fond of is an impostor. I've turned her out of the house,' seriously, how could I? And do you imagine she'd be contented with any excuse I could make to her for your disappearance? I can't risk it. You wouldn't want me to risk it. Come, you owe her a little consideration——!"

"Oh—!" she cried. "Yes"—but still she trembled.

Barnaby smiled down on her encouragingly. Apparently,—after that one quick word that had hushed her outcry,—he was unconscious of misconstruction.

"Besides," he said, "there will be row enough in the papers over my reappearance. I couldn't stand them getting hold of this. Good Lord! It would make us a laughing-stock."

"I am—sorry," she said, in a broken voice. Barnaby dropped his own.

"Don't be sorry," he said. "Be a brave girl, and let's keep it to ourselves."

Her heart jumped and stood still. She looked at him like some wild thing caught in a trap, without hope or help, crying its uttermost defiance.

And the man understood. His eyes looked straight into hers, blue and earnest, no longer careless.

"If I trust you," he said, "you must trust my honour. Please understand that I am a gentleman. We'll play our farce to stalls and the gallery, and when the curtain is down we'll treat each other with the most profound respect."

She tried to speak and could not. His voice softened.

"There's nothing else to be done," he said. "It won't be so hard on you;—you're an actress. And we'll find a way out, somehow. Perhaps, in a month or two, I can manage to have important business in America——"

She caught at that.

"And take me with you and drop me somewhere—?" she suggested.

"Take you with me and drop you somewhere?" he repeated. "Exactly. We must think it over."

"I could get killed in a railway accident—anything!" she said, in an eager, breathless voice.

"How accommodating!" said Barnaby. "There, that's settled. To my mother, and all outsiders, we'll be the most ordinary couple; but in private it shall be Sir and Madam. Shake hands on it, and promise me you'll play up."

He took her hands, the one with his ring on, the other bare. And Susan looked up at him, and was not afraid any more. She felt safe, and yet reckless;—almost as if she did not care at all how it ended, as if nothing were too dangerous, too adventurous for her to promise him.

"Right," he said. "And it's comedy, not tragedy, we're playing. We mustn't forget that."

"No," she said uncertainly; but she was not so sure.

"And now I'm going round to the stables," he said, changing his tone. But he turned back again on his way to the door.

"What am I to call you?" he asked. "The other lady had a string of fine-sounding names. Which of them do you go by?"

She coloured. His question smote her with the strangeness of their compact.

"Only one," she said, "and that was my own. I asked your mother to call me Susan."

"Susan," he said to himself. "Susan ... I'll remember."

She took one impetuous step towards him as he was going out.

"How good you are to me," she cried unsteadily. "Oh, how good you are!"

But Barnaby shook his head.

"Poor child," he said briefly. "I hope you'll always think I was good to you."

And he went out of the house whistling to himself.

*****

"What shocking writing!" said Lady Henrietta, "and how blotted! Who's your illiterate correspondent?"

Barnaby had stuffed his letter into his breast-pocket as he walked across the room.

"Julia," he said shortly.

As if upon second thoughts, he felt for it again, pulled it out, and tossed it into the fire. Its agitated, irregular lines started out black on the burning pages. Susan, who was sitting on the velvet curb, turned away her face that she might not read.

Lady Henrietta, frail but indomitable, throned upon her sofa, eyed her son jealously.

"How did she know so quickly?" she asked.

"She heard it from somebody, I suppose," said Barnaby. "Why, mother, do you imagine a real live ghost can visit Leicestershire without the whole county hearing? ... She wants me to go over and show myself."

"You're not going?"—her tone was sharp.

"No," he said. "I'll tell her I am under contract to exhibit myself exclusively at a music-hall.—And besides, I have to run up to London. I want to give old Dawson the fright he deserves. He must have been in a frantic hurry to wipe me out of his books. What on earth made you choose him to hunt for me?"

"Take Susan with you," said Lady Henrietta. "Go with him, my child, and don't let him out of your sight."

"I don't think she would like it," said Barnaby, doubtfully, but his mother was not to be gainsaid. It was almost as if the mention of Julia had revived a vague apprehension in her, as if she were afraid to let him go by himself. He submitted, laughing.

"Well," he said, "if you'll lend her your fur coat I'll wrap her in that and take her. We'll go up in the morning and come down at five;—and she can amuse herself getting clothes."

He bent down to Susan.

"If you don't mind," he said, half in a whisper; his tone was apologetic. "I think you had better come."

And so they went up together.

In the train he supplied her with an armful of picture papers, and she studied them gravely, hidden from him behind their outstretched pages, till they reached London, when she had to put down her screen. Once only he interrupted her.

"Look at that," he said.

The train was swinging on, making up time between Kettering and Luton; the letters danced as he held out his open newspaper, with a finger on the place. Its heading stared at her—"A LEICESTERSHIRE ROMANCE."

"That," said Barnaby, and his eyes twinkled—he had put away seriousness—"is all about you and me."

She did not see any more pictures after that, only bits of what she had read before he took back his paper and, turning over the crackling sheet, settled into his corner. Whatever she tried to look at, she saw only the printed column proclaiming the dramatic return of a well-known sportsman supposed to be dead; and at the bottom, where his thumb had pressed the paper, a touching reference to the subject's beautiful American wife....

At St. Pancras he put her carefully into a hansom and got in beside her.

"Now," he said, "this is our dress rehearsal. First, we must see about your theatrical wardrobe; that's the expression, isn't it? I'm going to take you to the woman my mother goes to, and while she is rigging you out I'll cut away to my lawyers, and see my own tailor; and then I shall fetch you and we'll have lunch. We shall have to get accustomed to each other."

Driving through the streets with him was curiously exhilarating. Perhaps her spirit was responsive to a reaction. After all, she was young.... If Barnaby knew, and did not condemn her, might she not for a short while dare to be light-hearted—leave the weight of it on his shoulders?

London had become a city of enchantment. She had passed through in the care of Lady Henrietta's messenger, at the end of her journey over the sea; and then she had felt tired and frightened, and she had looked listlessly out of the cab windows, thinking that if Fate betrayed her, she might find herself wandering friendless in these very streets. Now the dark ways were gilded....

"Here we are," said Barnaby, jumping out. "*Mélisande*. She's a great friend of ours, but she ruined herself racing, and started the shop as a different kind of gamble. Let's go up."

In the show-room upstairs two or three haughty ladies were trailing up and down, on view. The customers were not allowed to touch them; these sat round the room on the sun-faded yellow cushions, gazing at the models as if they were made of wax.

"Mélisande is uncommonly sharp," said Barnaby. He had walked in boldly and given his name to the presiding genius, who had simply glanced and vanished. "Do you see these creatures sweeping to and fro?"

"Yes," said the girl. "Poor things; they look very cross. I suppose they are dreadfully ill paid?"

Barnaby smothered an irreverent laugh.

"Paid?" he said. "Not a farthing. She introduces them in the season, and, in return, they have to act as dummies. They hate it; but she knows how to drive a bargain. It's a fine advertisement. Half the world comes to stare at the beauties—it's funnier than a picture gallery. And, of course, the pull of being taken up by Mélisande in her society capacity is enormous."

"Who are they?" asked Susan, puzzled.

"Oh, heiresses, of sorts, They used to be whisked away in their own motors at six o'clock. I daresay they are still," said Barnaby. "Here she is."

CHAPTER IV

An inner door flew open, and a stout woman with dark hair and clever, tired eyes, artistically blacked, appeared. She ran up to Barnaby and shook him, then let him go, and inspected him at all angles, with her head on one side as if he were a Paris model.

"Barnaby!" she screamed. "It is really Barnaby. You lunatic, I thought you were dead and buried."

"They all thought that," said Barnaby. "It's a bit rough on me."

"Let me pinch you again!" she said. "I can't have you in here if you're not alive. It's against all my rules, and customers are so timid. Of course, as a ghost you might be very useful. Make the brutes pay up!"

"What an eye to business!" he said, enduring her inspection.

"My dear man, I am in the workhouse! My friends insist on patronizing me, and ordering all kinds of magnificence, and then they go away imagining they have done me a kindness. I never dine out without meeting at least one frock that's a bad debt, and you can't be brilliant when you are being eclipsed by a wretch opposite out of your own pocket. But what do you want? I can't come out to lunch. I am rushed to death. There's an awful old Russian princess in there I can't get rid of. She says she wants to learn the trade, and I daren't leave her with my designs. I can't make out whether she's only a Nihilist or a kleptomaniac."

"I want to put my wife in your hands," said Barnaby. "I'll come for her at two. Can you burn all that crape, and dress her in something sensible?"

Mélisande screamed again, fixing her eyes for the first time on Susan.

"Is it a joke," she said, "or have you been playing fast and loose with other people?"

"I don't know what you mean," said Barnaby, but his eyes hardened. She glanced at his face, subduing her voice a little.

"I have never been paid," she said, "for an outfit of the most expensive mourning. The day after we read of your—departure in the papers, Julia Kelly came in here and asked what was the proper thing to wear when you lost your—love. I told her it varied. If the man hadn't proposed black would look like an affectation. I suggested mauve as harmlessly sentimental. And she said, 'But if he were practically your husband?' and I said, of course, practically widow's mourning, but not a cap. And she wore it...."

He moved restlessly under her detaining hand on his sleeve. "I'm betraying no confidences," she said. "It's a matter of common knowledge.—How long, in the name of goodness, have you been married? Who is she?"

"Two or three years," he said. She was still holding on to his coat.

"Wait," she said. "Wait. Oh, you are as mad as ever. How do you want her dressed? She looks awfully young, poor child."

But Barnaby had made his escape.

An hour later Susan looked at herself in the long mirrors that were all round her, and did not know herself any longer, she was so changed.

She had grown used to the deep black garments that seemed a part of her life. Far off and dimly she remembered the old family lawyer in shocked consultation with her nurses, his old-fashioned anxiety that when she was strong enough to travel she should be fittingly attired, and do honour to her sad estate....

A door opened at the other end of the room, and she saw Barnaby in the mirror, saw him standing petrified on the threshold till Mélisande's laugh called him to his senses.

"Do you like her?" said she. Susan did not hear what he said. But in the mirror he came towards her, and she turned round to meet him shyly.

"Take her away, then," said Mélisande. "Buy a shilling's-worth of violets and stick them in her coat; it's all that's lacking. I'll send down a trunk full of oddments with you to-night.—And give my compliments to Julia when you see her. 'To account rendered,' you can murmur in her ear."

Her malicious laugh pursued them a little way down the stairs. They came out into the street and walked along side by side.

"I went to see Dawson," said Barnaby suddenly. "Burst into his office, meaning to scare the old jackass out of his wits. He—he turned the tables on me. Made me feel a brute."

"How?" asked Susan.

He did not explain at once, engaged in making a way for her on the pavement. Then he answered briefly.

"He told me how he had found you."

His tone, angry as it was, warmed her soul.

"But,—it was not your business," she said, in a low voice. "It had nothing to do with you."

"I couldn't tell him that," said Barnaby. "Lord, how he went for me, poor old chap—! Spared me nothing. Said I could never make it up to you.... It's ridiculous, isn't it? But if you'd heard him attacking me!—I had to promise him I would try."

He was walking on beside her, so close that his arm brushed hers, his long strides falling in with her little steps. And he was looking down on her with a sort of raging kindness.

"You poor little girl!" he said.

They went on for awhile in silence, and then Barnaby stopped in his absent-minded progress. His good-humour was back, and the joke of this expedition was again uppermost in his head. He pointed with his stick at a strange and wonderful work of art in a milliner's window.

"Let's go in here and buy some of these hats," he said.

All her life Susan remembered that day with him. It was all so absurd, so simple. That strange town, London, was always to her the place where he and she made acquaintance, playing to ignorant audiences their game of Let's Pretend. She began to know him;—the way he walked, swinging his shoulders, stopping short when a sight amused him; his whimsical earnestness over little things, and the lines that came round his mouth when he smiled....

There were horses being put into the train when they arrived at St. Pancras. The grooms in charge of them were leading them gingerly through the people, past the lighted bookstall, persuading them up the gangways into their boxes. There was a small commotion as one of them, snorting, refused to step on the slanting boards. Tugging and shouting at him made him worse; he began to plunge, scattering the onlookers and the porters smiting his flanks.

"Hi! you infernal idiots..." said Barnaby. "Back him in."

He went over to the horse himself, and took hold of his bridle, turned him round, and walked him in like a lamb. Then, as the porters clapped shut the side of the horse-box, he waited to ask whose hunters were going down. Susan, lingering a little way apart, saw a big man with a cigar in his mouth spin round and seize him. Two or three more shot out of the throng and hurled themselves upon him, wringing his hand.

"It's Barnaby himself," they shouted. "Barnaby himself!"

They crowded him up the platform, a noisy escort, hiding their feelings under boisterous chaff; Meltonians, old acquaintances.... They passed by Susan, gossiping hard.

All at once Barnaby broke loose from them, turning back. "Great Joseph!" he said. "I've lost my wife!"

What if he had? What if she had cut the tangle, had slipped when his back was turned into one of these moving trains, and passed out of his life, out of the bustle into the throbbing darkness, like a match that had been lit and extinguished, leaving no trace?

She watched him hurrying back, looking for her; saw his quick glance along a glimmering line of carriages passing him on his left, and guessed his apprehension. Soon he was bearing down on her, charging through the press, and had pulled her hand through his arm.

"It was too bad, wasn't it?" he said. "I'm awfully sorry,—Susan."

There was a real relief in his voice. She felt it, wondering. Was he so glad to find her still his prisoner, his accomplice?

"Did you think," she said, and in her own voice laughter struggled with a strange inclination to tears,—"that I had run away?"

"Come on," he said cheerfully, not replying. "Hold on to me. Those chaps are looking at us."

He marched her to his friends, who had halted in a body when he dashed back, and waited, grinning sympathetically, for his return.

"Here is my wife," he said. "I brought her up to town to get rid of her widow's weeds."

They shook hands with her solemnly, a kind gravity in their manner to her subduing them for a minute; and then, as Barnaby settled her in the Melton slip, they hung round the carriage door, and their tongues were loosened.

"Where did you pick up these horses? Are they part of your baggage from another world?"

Barnaby laughed.

"They aren't mine," he said. "I brought nothing back with me, not even a collar-stud. Why, I pawned my watch in the States!"

"Wouldn't the ferryman let you return on tick? But you were mixed up with them, Barnaby, when I saw you. I'd know your voice anywhere, shouting Woa!"

"He's bound to get mixed up with horses, alive or dead," said the big man. "I tried to find out myself whose cattle they are, but the name is unintelligible. They can't pronounce it down there; not all the sneezing and snarling in the station can do it. I'll bet its another of these wild Austrians."

"D'you remember the three counts who set out on a slippery day to ride to the meet at Scalford;—and were fetched back to the Harboro', the three of them, half an hour afterwards, in a cart?"

"Broken ribs, wasn't it?" said Barnaby.

"Cracked heads, I fancy. I'll never forget the sight it was; all you could see of 'em was the three shiny top hats, stove in."

The lights were flickering in the station only the great yellow clock-face shone unchangeable, with its minute hand creeping up. Down below on the platforms scurrying passengers went their ways, gathering in thickening groups and eddying here and there round a pile of luggage. Everywhere there was restlessness.

Susan leant back in her corner. Their end of the platform was a little dim, and it was less frequented. She noticed a woman's figure passing along the train.

Barnaby was loitering, half in, half out of the door, absorbed in chatter. They were asking him if he were coming out with the Quorn, offering to lend him a crock to-morrow; relating the current news about men and horses. Once the big man turned his head casually as the figure that Susan had noticed passed. His mouth shaped itself in a whistle, but he made no remark. Only his broad back seemed to block out a little more of the view.

"It's about time we started," he said.

"What's the matter down there?" asked Barnaby.

"Oh, I fancied I saw a customer," he said promptly. "Did you take your wife to the grasping Mélisande? You might have patronized another old friend in me. There's a hat in the window I trimmed myself."

"What?" said Barnaby.

The big man chuckled heavily.

CHAPTER IV

"You didn't know I'd gone in for millinery?" he said. "If you had had your eyes about you you'd have seen my establishment. *There's* a business that women never will understand! They haven't got bold ideas; they are too fond of twisting. It was an accident, really. I was financing an aunt of mine, Clara Lady Kilgour,— and the thing was going bankrupt. I strolled into the shop one morning and found Clara weeping, and the Frenchy who had lured her into it sniffing like a noxious weed in a bed of artificial roses. Just by way of cheering her up a bit, I snatched up an affair the serpent was working at—a muddle of feathers and scraps of lace.— 'You'll ruin that!' they wailed. But hey, presto! I had found my vocation. I kicked out the bailiffs and took it over. And now I am running it as 'The Earl of Kilgour, late Fleur-de-lis.'"

The guard came down the train, shutting doors. Barnaby's friends dropped off, tumbling into the smoker behind. The whistle shrilled.

"Wouldn't you rather get in with them?" said Susan, in sudden shyness.

"What? that would never do," explained Barnaby, pulling up the window. "The poor dear fellows have left us religiously to ourselves."

He threw a *Westminster* on her knee and took off his hat.

"What was Kilgour staring at, do you know?" he asked. "He seemed rather disturbed; didn't want us to notice."

"I don't know," she said.

Barnaby laughed out loud.

"We got on famously," he declared. "We'd pass muster anywhere. But you are tired out, aren't you? Lean back in your corner and go to sleep."

The slip carriage was rocking from side to side, and her head ached from the strain and excitement of the day. The same shyness that had smitten her as his friends left them made her shut her eyes under his regard. She rested her head on the stiff padding, listening to the thrum of the engine, wandering in dreams that could not match the fantastic unlikeliness of what had befallen; and all the while feeling his gaze on her.

She was roused by the jar as the train stopped at Bedford. The carriage door was opened and closed; they were no longer by themselves.

"Barnaby!"

Tears were imminent in the emotional Irish voice.

"How do you do, Julia."—The man's tone was firm and hard.

"I knew you were in the train.... But with these gossiping wretches all round you!—I could not bear to meet you with them...."

"Don't waken my wife. She's tired."

His warning struck abruptly on her impulsive murmur. She sat down, rustling, unfastening the furs at her throat. The train had started again, and was speeding on.

In her far corner Susan stirred. This was the figure she had seen in the distance, the figure that Barnaby's friend had tried to block out from his attention. All Barnaby's friends must guess how hard it would be for him to meet her again, since he had once worshipped her.... Looking straight into the flying darkness, Susan tried not to see his profile reflected in it, tried not to watch his expression, inscrutable as it was.

"What fools we were!" sighed Julia.

"Regular fools," he said.

The girl drew a quick breath. She had thought she was beginning to know him, and still she could not guess if he spoke in irony or despair. She raised her head; fluttered the paper on her knee.—They must not think that she was asleep. And Barnaby looked at her.

"This is an old friend of mine, Susan," he said sedately. Julia presented a pale face and shining eyes.

"Mrs. Hill must be quite accustomed to the enthusiasm of your friends," she said. "*I* have been lingering at St. Pancras since three o'clock,—somebody told me you had been seen in a restaurant—for the sake of travelling back with you."

"How good of you," said Barnaby, in the same constrained way. "We didn't know, did we, Susan, that we had been spotted?"

Julia turned to him again; her speaking eyes hardly left him.—"Not good," she said, "only human."

The train rocked on, filling the inevitable pause with its throbbing. Then Barnaby's voice cut into the silence.

"We don't mind indulging your human curiosity, Julia," he said, "but why stare at us so hard? We, too, are only human, aren't we, Susan?"

"It is so strange," said Julia, "to think of you with a wife."

Barnaby bit his lip. He reddened. Perhaps the sight of her had shaken him, had hit him deeper than he was willing to betray. Her emotion at meeting the man whom she had mourned as dead was visible; she made no attempt to hide it. Perhaps his own was the greater for being stifled by his determined effort at self-control. He got up, fiddling with the window-sash.

"Would you like this a bit down?" he said. "How is your headache?"

Did he know that her head ached, or had he addressed her at random? The girl felt an unreasonable anger at his ostentatious solicitude. Was he playing her off against his old love? Did such bitterness wait behind their compact? For the first time, his kindness hurt her. All a farce, all a blind, and a make-believe....

CHAPTER V

In the morning Barnaby went out hunting. He started gaily, in old clothes, on a borrowed horse.

"Next time I die," he said, "and they put away my relics, I beg you all not to scatter infernal white knobs of poison among them to keep away the moths. I call it irreverent. And unless this horrible smell wears off I'll have to keep to leeward. A single whiff of it would kill the scent."

He came in at dusk, stiff and splashed, but contented, calling for tea, and waking up the house. It was extraordinary what a difference his presence made as he limped into the hall and hung up his whip. Life and vigour seemed to blow in with him; the terriers rushed at him dancing, barking, pattering into the library at his heels. Lady Henrietta, propped on her sofa, gave a little sharp sigh.

"Give him his tea, Susan," she said briskly. "How did he carry you, Barnaby? Who was out?"

"Oh, all the world and his wife," he said. "Carry me? He wouldn't have carried a grasshopper. But I changed on to a chestnut that Rivington wants to sell. I've bought him. Not much to look at, but he goes well enough, and I was so pleased to feel a real galloper under me, I'd have given him any price.... It's good to be here again. Though my boots are as hard as iron. I believe I am lamed for life. By the by, Susan, I've let you in for one thing. I couldn't help it."

She looked up, startled, from her place by the fire.

"It's only to dine out with some people to-morrow night," he said, noticing her alarm. "I couldn't get out of it, really; they mobbed me so."

"Who is it?" asked Lady Henrietta.

"Only the Drakes," said Barnaby.

His mother nodded. "Yes; show her off to your friends!" she said.

She was in and out of Susan's room next evening all the while she was dressing, and when the girl's toilet was finished she came with her hands full of jewel-cases.

"You can't wear much to-night," she said.

"It would look dressed up. But a few pins,—and a star or two to give you confidence in yourself.... My dear, you don't know what a help it is! And all the women you'll meet have been at one time or another in love with Barnaby. Hold up your head, and don't let them make you wretched. Is that you, Barnaby? I want you."

Barnaby passed by on his way from his own room, and her shrill call stopped him. His step outside sent the colour into Susan's cheek, and his voice came doubtfully through the door.

"Yes, mother?"

"Come in; come in. How shy you are!" said she, and the handle turned.

"You will tire yourself," he said, but she brushed aside his remonstrance.

"Rubbish!" she said. "I have the whole evening to lie up and swallow physic. Come here and stick these in for me, will you? Margaret is so clumsy."

"I beg your pardon," he said, under his breath, as he bent down, fulfilling his office.—"The exigencies of the piece must excuse me."

"What a queer way of apologizing for running a pin into your wife!" said his mother sharply. She might have been trusted to overhear. He had straightened himself, and was withdrawing rather precipitately, when his eyes fell on his own picture above the chimney-piece. "What is that thing doing here?" he asked, off his guard.

Lady Henrietta desisted from her pleased contemplation of Susan decked out with jewels.

"Well!" she said. "Of all things! Do you mean to say?—It has been there ever since she came. I had it hung there myself to be company for your heart-broken widow."

"Anyhow, we'll have it down now," he said hastily. "You'd rather not have the daub glaring at you, wouldn't you, Susan?"

Lady Henrietta turned her back on him.

"Don't mind him, my dear," she said. "We'll keep it."

There was warmth in her tone. She squeezed the girl's arm, bidding her remember that none of Barnaby's old flames could hold a candle to her. Somehow or other he had fallen under her displeasure.

"I'm afraid my acting doesn't come up to yours," he said, when they were shut into the motor. "My mother thinks I am too undemonstrative ... that I am unworthy of my good luck."

"Don't!" she said.

He laid his hand comfortingly on hers.

"Look here, little girl," he said. "It's no use taking things hard. We have to make the best of it. It won't last for ever.... We must look at the funny side of it. That's the bargain."

The swift drive through the night was already over. Three men, pushing aside the servants, were slapping Barnaby on the back. They bore a family likeness to each other, big men, with creased red necks, and short, rumpled sandy hair.

CHAPTER V

"Come along in," they cried heartily. "The house is full of old friends wanting to get at you,—and nothing but odds and ends for dinner."

But one of them managed to lower his hearty voice a trifle.—"You won't mind meeting Julia Kelly? She has asked herself for the night."

"Who else?" said Barnaby, in his ordinary tones.

"Kilgour and the Slaters and Rackham and the Duchess;—and a few more," reeled off his host, thankfully dropping the awkward subject now he had got out his warning. He rushed them into the house, and Susan was bewildered by the tumult that greeted them, the sea of unknown faces. Men and women alike were seizing on Barnaby and exclaiming. She hardly realized that they were at the same time taking stock of her. The three Drakes stood near her like a bodyguard, kind and stolid, settling into their usual phlegmatic form; and she felt glad of them.

"Getting on all right?" said Barnaby, as she passed him on her way in to dinner, and she smiled back at him.

He and she were not near each other; but once or twice he looked her way, bending his head and slewing half round to catch a glimpse of her; that—or else Lady Henrietta's stars, kept up her courage. She listened politely, not understanding much, to the local gossip running along the table.

"Have you picked up any horses yet, Barnaby? Sims has one or two going up on Saturday, at Leicester."

"I can let you have a bay, a capital fencer——"

"Oh, you don't palm off your roarers on me. I heard him to-day," said Barnaby.

"Well, I don't deny that he makes a noise——"

"I suppose you think I've been in the wilds so long I don't know a horse from a hedgehog!" said Barnaby. "Can anyone tell me what became of a black mare I had four seasons ago?"

"Do you mean Black Rose?" said Kilgour.

"That's the one. Do you know who has her?"

"I have," said Kilgour. "I took her from Peters. The fellow couldn't ride her. You can have her back if you want her, Barnaby; she isn't up to my weight. I remember you rode her at Croxton Park."

"And won," said Barnaby. "Want her? Rather."

Kilgour chuckled heavily.

"She isn't as young as she was, mind," he said. "But she can go still. I suppose you're not as keen as you used to be on breaking your neck?"

"As keen as ever," said Barnaby, with conviction.

"Does your wife ride?"

The question sounded maladroit; it was inconceivable that Barnaby should have married a wife who did not. His hesitation was singular in their eyes; they all stopped to listen.

"I really don't know," he said.

In the general burst of laughter Susan caught his glance of amused consternation. In that hard-riding company his ignorance was incredible. Men, having a curious predilection towards the unsuitable in wives, he might, after all, have committed that inconceivable piece of folly. Barnaby's wife might lamentably turn out incapable of sitting on a horse. But that Barnaby should not know—!

It was while they were all laughing at him that Susan became aware of Julia Kelly.

She was on the same side of the table as herself, placed far from the lion of the occasion; and was leaning her elbows on the table, looking full at Susan. The man between them was sitting back in his chair roaring helplessly at the joke.

"What an ignorant husband, Mrs. Hill," said Julia, and her musical voice vibrated through the laughter. "Do you ride?"

"I have ridden," said Susan quietly. It was difficult for her to blot the memory of an encounter that the other woman ignored.

"But not with him?"

Mrs. Drake, springing up, made diversion.

"Why not have a steeplechase?" she cried.

She was one of these little women, all skin and bone, who cannot bear inaction, and whose wishes are carried out.

"Cross country," she said, silencing a growl from her husband. "You can ride the point-to-point course. We'll send round and tell everybody, and get them all here by twelve. And we'll put grooms with lanterns to mark the jumps."

The men jumped up, enthusiastic. The idea was just mad enough to appeal to their sporting instincts. In about three minutes the dining-room was deserted, and five motors were humming into the darkness to apprise and rally all who were reckless enough to join. In a neighbourhood always ready for a frolic there was no danger of the inspiration falling flat.

Barnaby himself was in the thick of it, mapping out preliminaries with the other men in the hall. The women clustered together, almost hysterical with excitement. And Susan drifted apart from the chattering circle, feeling outside it all.

She heard a gruff voice in her ear, and started. The tall, gaunt, hard-faced Duchess was standing over her.

"How are you getting on?" she said.

"It is a little strange to me," said Susan.

"But you are not moping," said the Duchess. "I can see you are made of better stuff. They are all mad, of course, but nobody will get hurt, if that is what you are afraid of."

CHAPTER V   41

Yes, that must be what she was afraid of, what inspired her with an undefined wretchedness. If she had been what they thought her, surely she would be feeling nervous. She was glad she had not made the mistake of pretending to be gay.

"I am an old friend of your husband's," said the Duchess, "—and he has asked me to be kind to you. I shan't warn you to beware of Julia; all the rest of them will, if they haven't already;—but I don't call that kindness."

"Barnaby asked you to be kind to me?" repeated Susan; she could not keep the wistfulness out of her voice; she had been thinking herself so utterly forgotten.

"Yes. It isn't the fashion here for husbands to worry about their wives, but he is a bit old-fashioned. I told him I'd come and talk to the little fish out of water. It is just a strange pond, my dear, and you'll soon begin swimming."

The clash of voices grew more uproarious in the hall. A man put his head in and vanished, looking for somebody. His brief appearance made the contrast between the excitement out there and this empty room more emphatic.

"I must get out of this," said the Duchess, switching her train as she rose from the sofa. "Kitty will have to lend me a habit and one of her husband's coats. I shall ride. There's a brook jump where there'll be trouble, and I want to see the fun. You had better drive with Kitty. I'll see to it. Have you anything warm to put on?"

Her caution was hardly equal to her good nature, and the clamour in the hall hardly drowned her indignant voice as she seized on a confidant in the doorway.

"I like her pluck. She's terrified to death, of course, but she doesn't look woe-begone. We must seem a pack of dangerous lunatics.... Where do these Americans get their spirit?"

"You don't read history, do you, Duchess?"

"Why?"

The man she had seized laughed shortly, amused at her bewildered face.

"Oh," he said, "we English are frightfully cock-a-hoop over our pedigrees. We don't remember it's they who are condescending to us. There's bluer and better blood across the Atlantic than any of ours, and it isn't smirched. They don't boast. They don't remind us of our blotted scutcheons.—We to talk of race!"

"What on earth do you mean, Kilgour?" said the Duchess. "Half of them are Huns and Finns, and the scum of Europe."

The big man was leaning against the door-post; his bantering tongue took on a sudden heat.

"A few," he said. "But the rest—! Scum, Duchess?—We're the dregs. There's not one of our great families that isn't mixed with the blood of traitors; that hasn't at one time or another sold its honour or stained its sword. Scots and English, all that was best of us once, are there, handing their valour down. After Culloden the country was drained of its gentlemen. Why, you can still hear the Highland tongue in South Carolina.... *They* went into exile while we hugged our estates and truckled to an usurper. And the soul of a country is the soul of its heroes.... Oh, I believe in race!—Let the rest of us take a pride in our tarnished titles and wonder at the fineness of strangers who are descended from the men who lost all for the sake of honour and loyalty to their King!"

The Duchess dropped her blunt voice into a lower key.

"Poor old Kilgour," she said. "You're thinking of that little brute Tillinghame and his dollar princess."

"Well!" he said, between his teeth. "You've only to look at them!—And his people sneer at her for aspiring to bear an illustrious title that began in dishonour, and has been dragged a few hundred years in the mud—!"

The Duchess moved away from the door; she had remembered Susan.

"I wish you'd capture Barnaby and send him in to his wife," she said. "He has forgotten that she exists.... I've had to make up a message.... I couldn't stand the dumb wistfulness in her face. It's a foolhardy business."

"I've just sent for Black Rose," said Kilgour, in his ordinary tone. "He was keen to ride her." He raised his voice. "—Here, Barnaby, you're wanted!"

But the messengers were returning already, and strange cars were dashing up. The hubbub was at its height. It was impossible to win Barnaby's attention. He turned his head impatiently as Kilgour made a grab at him.

"What is it now?" he said. "Oh, don't bother me, there's a good fellow. They want to settle how—Jim, Jim, is that you? Have you brought the horses?"

He ran down the steps.

A clatter of hoofs was audible in the darkness, and a groom, riding one horse and leading another pulled up below the steps, steadying his charges as they flung up their bewildered heads, blinking, kicking up the gravel.

"Ah, my beauty!" said Barnaby, in the voice of a lover. "Did you think I was dead?"

"Is that Black Rose?" called one of the men crowding to the door. "Wasn't she sold?"

"She was. But I'll have her back," he shouted up to them, rubbing the mare's dark head. "To the half of my kingdom I'll buy her back!"

The women, wrapped thickly, and disguised in furs, were streaming into the hall. Julia Kelly, who had lingered to the last, and was not yet ready, rushed down impulsively to his side.

"Oh, Barnaby, is that Black Rose? Dear thing, is she there? Oh, Barnaby—!"

Her voice thrilled and sank; she stretched out her hand, patting the mare's neck, rejoicing with him.

"It's like old times, isn't it?" he said.

The night wind ruffled his bare head, kissed a wisp of Julia's lace and blew it against him. She might have been forgiven for thinking his thick utterance was for her. The little scene, to all present who knew their tale, was romantic.

CHAPTER V

Kitty Drake looked over her shoulder in a funny, conscience-stricken way; the Duchess was poking her in the back, and at the same time interposing her rugged presence between romance and Susan. In a minute the girl was shielded by an oddly-sympathizing bevy of women, fussing over her in a transparent hurry to see that she was wrapped up warm.

The stable clock behind the house was beginning to strike, and the men who had been dining there had disappeared to change. Nobody was measuring the length of that interview.... At last Barnaby came in three steps at a time, a portmanteau in his arms.

"I say, Kitty; where can I go and dress?"

She looked at him severely over Susan's head.

"Run in anywhere," she said, and he pursued his impetuous way upstairs. Julia reappeared by herself, on her face what Kitty Drake stigmatized as a maddening consciousness.

"They say they are going to ride in their shirt-sleeves," she said, "but that will hardly make them visible. It's nearly pitch dark outside."

"They are idiots," said Kitty Drake. "Fancy Gregory calling to us when we were upstairs to know if we would lend them our night-dresses. I told him I was too thrifty."

"Why not?" said Julia. "Barnaby can have mine."

A blank pause saluted her speech, and then, with one accord, the women began to acclaim the notion as if it were the most ordinary thing in the world. Even Kitty, in her haste to dissipate the impression that Julia's declaration might make on the girl beside her, caught up the idea and made it hers. She flew up and down arranging.

"A bit mediæval, isn't it?" said Kilgour, watching the riders as they struggled with gossamer raiment that sometimes flopped over their heads unassisted, and sometimes clung, entangling them in cobwebs. — "In the days of knighthood we all wore bits of our ladies' clothing."

The Duchess grumbled.

"Pity we can't revive other habits," she said. "There was a useful practice of wringing obnoxious people's necks."

"Poor Julia," said Kilgour. "Don't grudge her her little triumph. She only wants to publish it abroad that it was her own fault she was forsaken."

But the Duchess's brow was grim.

The night was black and starless, and had been still. The villages they passed gave back startled echoes, awakened out of sleep by the rattling of the cavalcade. Susan was tucked in between Kitty Drake and the Duchess, who intended to change to her horse when the race began, and in the meantime was driving them at a smacking pace. She kept her buggy at the head of the procession, and was the first to whisk round a perilously sudden turning that led off the turnpike, and sent them bumping into a field.

In front of them stretched a dim line of country that had darkened into strangeness, puzzling the most familiar eyes. Here and there were flickering lights, like will-o'-the-wisps, luring and warning, indicating danger. And the men were to ride there....

Susan stood up in the buggy, supported by Kitty's arm, straining her eyes to watch the start. She could make out a little; by dint of hard gazing she learnt to distinguish the figures that moved yonder. In the middle of the field an indistinct line of riders were drawn up, waiting.

A man shouted back to the watchers, and their prattle hushed. There was an instant of absolute silence, suspended breath;—and then somebody swung a lantern.

"Go!" he cried.

Leaping into the darkness the line of horses broke like a wave and went, their limbs gleaming. Already they were blundering into the first hedge, and there was a crash, relieved by laughter as the first spill resulted in one man picking himself up unhurt. The rest were swinging on; rising again, more warily, a little farther; and just visible, for the last time, black objects against the sky.

The Duchess set her foot in the stirrup and galloped off. Susan rocked as she stood, and was nearly flung out as the buggy started forward, and the whole cavalcade whirled blindly into a lane that was all ruts and stones and turf.

Strange what an unimagined wildness darkness and ignorance lent to that plain strip of country. The fields that slanted were dreadful hills sinking into unknown abysses, the brooks rushed like rivers, the hedges lifted themselves gigantic. Many who had ridden over the ground by daylight times without number exclaimed, and wished the night at an end.

Kitty Drake, however, was screaming with delight.

"Here they come!" she shrilled. "Oh, shut up, you people. You'll scare the horses. I know it's awfully weird, but still—! That's Dicky, of course. I'd know Nanny's frills anywhere; he looks like a mad pierrot. Oh, and Colonel Birch, with Mrs. Uffington's chiffon scarf tied on to him. Mrs. Uffington, it was base of you not to risk it. My best garment is floating there, being torn to ribbons by Gregory's spurs."

"Sit down, Kitty!" cried somebody at her elbow. "You can't see anything yet; it's all imagination."

"I see it with my mind's eye," she declared; but subsided.

A few men on horseback scampered out of the nothingness and drew up beside them. This was the place to watch the riders jump the water. They pressed close in a peering bunch, the cigars in their mouths making red points in the gloom. The Duchess halted by the buggy, a curious figure in Gregory Drake's greatcoat, with the sleeves turned up.

CHAPTER V

"All right, so far," she said, in her gruff voice, cheerily. "They have been signalling with the lanterns. Queer how the darkness seems to swallow 'em up alive!"

As she spoke they all heard a distant thudding. There was something terrifying in this invisible approach; it seemed to promise catastrophe. Surely some sudden end would come to that beating of horses' hoofs—! Nearer and nearer the unseen racers came, until they were almost on the top of the watching throng. Then there was a glimpse of great beasts rising in the air.

The first horse came down short of the landing-place, plunging into the hidden water that ran beneath. His splash was followed by another as the next man faltered and went in deep. Then a third went up.

Someone had an acetylene motor lamp, and held it suddenly on high. It made a vivid glare, illuminating that rider's face, his eyes staring ahead, his mouth shut and smiling——

"Turn out that lamp. You'll dazzle 'em, you damned idiot!" yelled Kilgour. "It isn't a pantomime!"

The next horse had taken fright. There was stamping and swearing; and then the blinding flare was extinguished, leaving the scene darker. The faces that had shone pale and unearthly in that brief wave of limelight could not longer be recognized.

Susan shivered with excitement. That was Barnaby she had seen....

No woman was in his head just then; his spirit was intent on the splendid peril of that night ride. Something in herself understood him. She felt proud of him, reckless with him, afraid of nothing. But he had landed and was away on the farther side.

Now they were all in or over, and the water jump was deserted. The last who had failed to clear it had struggled up the bank and swung dripping into his saddle, feeling for his reins. They were laughing at him because he had let go and tried to swim, not at first realizing that it wasn't up to his knees....

But he had lost his head in the dark.

There was time, if they hurried, to reach the hillside at the back of the intervening dip, full of pitfalls, and gain a place of vantage to witness what they might of the finish. Kilgour, who knew the country blindfold, pushed on ahead, guiding them; and the rest trusted to his instinct. He unlatched a gate, flinging it wide for the others to scramble through, cut along close under the branching side of a spinney, forded a water-course, and spun up a cart track; emerging suddenly on the side of the hill. Behind him pressed a clattering, jolting troop, that stopped dead as he threw up his arm and listened.

The riders had to make a circuit, but they should be near. What was the meaning of this long pause? of the utter silence? For the first time the women betrayed a nervous thrill that was not pure excitement. The waiting dashed their spirits. They tried to laugh, and their laughter sounded strange.

"There's bound to be some misfortune," muttered someone, as a night bird croaked in the trees. And above the hush a woman's voice pealed, hysterical, calling on heaven to witness that she had dissuaded Billy— —

"Hush!"

The men who were judging talked in whispers as they sat quietly on their horses, motionless, save for an occasional jingling bit, under the clump of firs that was the winning-post. Their ears were on the alert, but all the queer noises of the night were treacherously alike, and that might be nothing but running water that seemed a distant galloping. One man looked at his watch.

"They're due," he said. "Bar accidents. Can't you hear 'em?"

Then at last, clear in the distance, the gallop came.

Far in that mysterious valley the lanterns twinkled, making the darkness visible. Where the lights glimmered there was danger.

"D'you see that?" said Kilgour in the ear of his neighbour. A spark dipped suddenly.—"One man down."

At the next jump another light went out.

"A bit weird, these signals," said Kilgour's neighbour. "I don't like 'em; it's too infernally suggestive. Where are they now?"

The watchers herded together, all standing up, all staring; trying to pierce the gloom, as the unseen horses came thundering up the rise. Singly they ran in.

Susan was sure that Barnaby would win. She could not understand why her heart beat so loud.

"One—two—three—!"

They were all frantically counting. Five men still up;—but not yet near enough to distinguish faces.

"If Barnaby isn't in the first three he's down."

Who said that? She gave one shudder and was quite still.

"Oh, God, don't let him be killed. Don't let him be killed!" she was crying to herself.

The fir trees spread their dark plumes overhead; in the boughs there was a strange sighing.... If he was not in the first three, if he was missing—her one friend in a land of strangers, lying there crushed and lifeless in the dark:—

"Oh God—!" she cried under her breath.

And then out of the blackness shot a headlong figure, cleaving it like an arrow. That blur beneath was the final jump, the last hedge that barred the way with its ragged line. And he charged it as if it were not there, keeping on in his tremendous rush.

"Barnaby!" they shouted. They knew his laugh before they could see his face.

"A near thing," he said, and pulled up the black mare, who turned her head towards him as he dismounted, her eye-balls glistening in the darkness with some-

CHAPTER V   47

thing like human pride.

"You didn't steady her there," said Kilgour.

"Steady her?—We had to come for all we were worth!" he said.

The Duchess, striding afoot, made her way into the circle round him. Barnaby was explaining how he had ridden into one of the lantern-bearers, a silly fool who had turned his light and was standing into the hedge; and how he had got off to make sure the poor devil wasn't injured. He had had to ride after that like fury; no leisure to grope his way....

"Since you are not smashed up," said the Duchess, shaking him by the arm, "go and show yourself to your wife. You nearly frightened her to death."

She piloted him to the buggy, and stood by, with her unsentimental countenance considerately averted.

"I am so glad you won," said Susan. She spoke steadily, controlling the traitorous catch in her throat. How was she to assure him that she was not guilty of causing him to be dragged to her side?

The man smiled at her stiff politeness. He was still hot, still breathing a little hard, the spell of his ride still on him;—and Julia's wisp of muslin was twisted round his neck.

"I'm sorry you were scared," he said. "I'm rather in the habit of doing ridiculous things like this. There wasn't much danger really ... and I didn't think you would mind."

His casual apology struck her like a blow. What right had she—? How it must amuse him that she should affect to care.

"I did not mind," she said proudly. "It was—funny."

One of his friends was coming up with a coat to throw over him. The men who had come to grief were straggling in, bruised and dirty, but miraculously sound. Kitty Drake leaned over the wheel on the other side, hailing them, calling to each man to ask if he was alive....

"Was it?" said Barnaby, and smiled. The glint in his eyes reminded her of his face as the light flashed on him, dare-devil, reckless, down there when he jumped the water.

Perhaps the joke was a little too much for him.

"You are not altogether a callous person," he said slowly. "I don't believe you, Susan. You fainted when I came home...."

CHAPTER VI

"Dull?" said Lady Henrietta.

The girl became aware of her with a start.

Barnaby had just gone, and the house was quiet. Late as usual, he had come clinking down in his spurs, and run out to his waiting horse; and she had seen him off, but had not yet turned away from the door. Lady Henrietta's uncommon earliness had surprised her. She did not know how wistful her aspect was.

"No," she said. "Oh no. I was only watching——"

"To see the last of him," retorted Lady Henrietta smartly. "I know—I know. One glimpse of him as he crosses the wooden bridge, and again a peep before he cuts across by the willows. How dare you let him set off day after day without you?"

She paused. There was mischief in her eye, an unwonted touch of excitement. One would have said she was plotting.

"You are too lamb-like," she said. "I'll give you a horse. Tell him you'll go hunting with him to-morrow."

She laughed outright at the girl's look of consternation.

"No," she said, "you wouldn't. My dear, you have got him, and you must keep him. It's a woman's business to look after her husband, to throw herself into his occupations, and rescue him from the ravening lions that run up and down in the earth. Why didn't you back me up when I attacked him last night, and he put me off with his nonsense about a quiet pony? Why didn't you insist?"

Susan flushed scarlet, remembering Lady Henrietta's unexpected onslaught and Barnaby's good-humoured amazement; his vague promise of giving her a riding lesson. He glanced at her mirthfully, and that look of his had called up a hot disclaimer of any wish. Was it not in their bargain that as far as possible they were not to haunt each other?

"Since you are so meek," said Lady Henrietta, who did not miss her confusion, "*I* must put my finger in the pie."

Her eyes were not young, but they were far-seeing; she turned from the prospect at which Susan had been gazing, and laid authoritative fingers on her sleeve.

"Run upstairs," she said, "and get into your habit. I've told Margaret to have it ready. It won't fit, probably, but you are not vain;—it's borrowed. Don't stare at me, you baby! Rackham and I settled it the night he dined here, while you and

Barnaby were trying not to talk to each other. I don't know whether you can ride or not, but you must begin."

She finished up with a chuckle. The sight of Susan's face—well, that was enough for her. She had turned a more potent key than she knew.

Two horses were pawing the gravel beside the door, and one of them had a side-saddle on his back. She had seen them coming when she despatched her daughter-in-law to dress. Rackham himself was waiting on the steps. Lady Henrietta beckoned to him with the joy of a bad child firing a train of powder.

"I've told her," she said. "She'll be down in a minute. Take her once or twice round the park, and if she doesn't fall off——"

"She won't fall off," said Rackham.

"You brought her a quiet horse?"—the conspirator was feeling a slight compunction.

Barnaby's cousin, his ancient rival, smiled under his moustache. "I'll take good care of her, my aunt," he said.

"You are an obliging demon, Rackham," she observed. "It was good of you to give up your hunting."

"They'll be at Ranksboro' about twelve," he said significantly. "If you really wanted us to give Barnaby a surprise——"

Lady Henrietta favoured him with an enlightening nod. Whether or no he was bent on furthering her purposes, assuredly she might trust him.

"Villain," she said. "You understand me; it's an experiment,—it's a squib!"

Twice Susan rode solemnly round the park. To her, remembering how, as a child, she had ridden, cross-legged, bare-backed, anyhow, anything—their solicitude was absurd. She swung her foot in the stirrup, lifting a transfigured face.

"*You* are all right," said Rackham, glancing backwards towards the distant windows. "I knew you could ride."

He bent over in his saddle to unlatch the hand-gate that Barnaby had ridden through before them, taking his short cut over the wooden bridge by the willows. Keeping his horse back, he held it open.

"Come out this way," he said. They went cantering up the lane.

Dim and dark was the landscape, threatening rain, and the clouds were sinking lower and lower, rubbing out the hills. A kind of expectation hung in the air. A storm gathering perhaps. They rode up and up, until the narrow green lane came to a sudden stop, and a break in the high barriers of hawthorn let them on to a ridge that hung over a wide sweep of valley. Underneath lay a fallow strip, reddish brown amidst the green waves of pasture, and a party of rooks rose cawing above the idle plough.

Susan, her heart still dancing, laid a happy hand on her horse's mane,—the willing horse that carried her so smoothly.

"You like it?" said Rackham.

There was a subtle difference between his guardianship and that of his cousin. She missed that queer sense of security that she had with Barnaby. Why, she knew not, but Rackham's neighbourhood troubled her. She felt a nervous inclination to burst into hurried chatter.

"It was awfully kind of Lady Henrietta to arrange it,—and of you," she said; "though you were both afraid that I should disgrace you. Yes, you were watching;—and she too: her mind misgave her when she saw me in the saddle.—What is the matter with the horses?"

"Look!" he said, smiling broadly.

And immediately she guessed. Far on the right she distinguished a flick of scarlet.

"Oh!" she said, in an awed whisper, understanding.

"That's one of the whips riding on," he explained; "they are going to draw the spinney down there, just underneath. We're in for it, aren't we?—Shall we stay where we are, and chance Barnaby's displeasure? I'll open the gates for you, and give you a lead. Can you jump?"

She laughed at him, carried out of herself, back in remote adventures when there had been nothing she would not dare. Her blood was up, and she felt her horse quivering beneath her. Hounds were in the spinney; she had glimpses of dappled bodies ranging among the trees; at the eastern side an interminable troop of riders were pouring into the field. There seemed no limit to their numbers as they massed thicker and thicker on the skirts of the cover till there was but the south side clear.

"Keep still!" said Rackham in a breath, and as he whispered a living flash passed by. It vanished across the fallow, as a whistle shrilled from below. One of the whips had seen him.

"Steady!" said Rackham. "Hounds are coming out. He broke at that bottom corner.—Now!"

Her horse bounded away with his. She was close behind him as they raced down the headland. The fence at the end was low; a thorn-crammed ditch and a rotten rail. She took it, hardly knowing, but for her horse's excitement, that she had jumped. He broke into a gallop then, and she let him go.

"Who's the lady out with Rackham?" called one man, waiting his turn at a gap. The man ahead of him squeezed through before replying.

"Don't know. She's chosen a damn reckless pilot!"

But no man's recklessness could have beaten hers. She followed him blindly; nothing daunted her, nothing dimmed the eagerness in her soul. This was to live indeed.

They were hard on the pack. She could hear them in front, could sometimes catch a view of them flickering on. A great noise of galloping filled the air behind, drumming hard; but she was still keeping her lucky place in the van. She and Rackham....

There was something formidable ahead. She felt her horse faltering in his stride, not afraid, but doubtful;—those that were close behind were parting right and left; some of them were falling back. Without turning her head she knew it. Recklessly she kept on. The others might blench.... She would not.

Up went her horse, and in mid-air she had time to ask herself what would happen, to guess that it was touch and go. It seemed a great while before they came down, with a jar and a stagger, galloping rather wildly on.

She was too excited still to feel tired, too ignorant of danger to know what a wild line she was taking now. Just ahead of her Rackham had disappeared with a crack of timber, and she must not be left behind.

An ominous crash pursued her as she went through a stiff barrier of thorns; a loose horse was flying past. She looked dizzily for Rackham, wondering if it was his. It tried to clear the next fence riderless, but was too unsteady, and swerving crosswise, nearly brought her down. In the field beyond it was stopped by an oxer. Someone behind cracked his whip....

"We've beaten the lot!" called Rackham; his voice came a little hoarse in her ear. "Half of 'em funked that bullfinch, and there's one fellow in the ditch——"

She reeled in her saddle.

"I've—no—breath left," she panted.

"Pull up. Pull up!" said Rackham, and leaned over as she managed to stop her horse. Her knees trembled and she held on a minute; she thought she was going to fall off out of sheer fatigue.

Hounds were baying on the other side of the hedge. They had got their fox. People were coming up on all sides, in haste to mingle with the few who had ridden straight. She was vaguely conscious of their interested regard; she heard a general buzz of gossip.

"There's Barnaby," said Rackham. He had dismounted, and stood by her horse's shoulder, pretending to do something with a buckle, but in reality waiting for her to recover. His arm was ready to catch her if she should slide off; his wild eyes were fixed on her.

"Don't forget it was with me, not with him, you rode your first run," he said. The triumph in his whisper made her afraid. She felt like a truant.

What would Barnaby think of her? Would he be very angry? Had he watched her riding, wondering who she was? She lifted her face, a little proud, but troubled. All at once her glorious adventure wore the look of an escapade.

He had ridden up, but he was not looking at her at all. The set of his mouth was hard.

"I'll take charge of my wife," he said.

How strange it sounded. Would she never get used to it? She had an immediate sense of protection, of happiness out of all reason. But what else could he call her, before the world?

His cousin grinned at him brazenly.

"If you haven't too much on your hands," he said darkly. "Oh, take over your responsibilities if you like. You needn't fight me. It was your mother's idea.... But she's tired. She mustn't stop out too long."

"It was a mad thing to do," said Barnaby curtly; "risking her life over these fences—!"

"Come, come," said Rackham, "don't paint me too black. I took the greatest care of her. Didn't I?"

"I was looking on," said Barnaby.

He had turned to Susan at last, and she saw that his face was pale. Something in him responded to her look of rapture dashed.

"Poor little girl!" he said. "I didn't know—you cared about it—" Then he smiled ruefully. "By Jove!" he said. "You gave me a fright. I thought you'd get yourself killed a dozen times. And I had a bad start. I couldn't get up to you. There, don't let's look as if we were quarrelling, though under the circumstances,—do you think we should?"

She plucked up spirit to answer him in kind. "On the stage," she said, "the audiences would expect it."

"Well," he said, "we'll disappoint the audience.... You won your bet, Kilgour; it is my wife. Wasn't it wicked of her?"

She found herself trotting on at his side. Rackham had fallen back. It was Barnaby who directed her, who rode at her right hand; and a cheery crowd hemmed her in.

At the head of the procession hounds were moving on. Occasionally the authorities called a halt while they searched a patch of trees by the wayside, or turned aside to examine a hollow tree. But these were not serious diversions. Once, indeed, there was a whimper as the pack ran scampering into a small plantation, and the huntsman went in to see what it was, his scarlet glancing in the bare brown mist of larches.

"I know what'll happen to us," grumbled Kilgour, as the verdict was issued that it was empty. "We'll climb up on the top of Ranksboro' and the heavens will open on us."

The ranks closed up again as the pack tumbled back sadly into the road. Kilgour was a true prophet; they were bent at last towards that unfailing harbour. On they pushed, up hill and down, through a grey village where the trees shut out the sky from the winding street, and then slap in at a gate that let them on to the grass again.

"Where are we?" asked Susan, as she was squeezed in the press through the gate, finding elbow-room as her neighbours scattered on the other side, spreading

CHAPTER VI

downward.

"On the wild side of Ranksboro'," said Barnaby. "Stick to me if you are thinking of getting lost. You'll see where you are when we reach the top, and you can look down on the cover;—but that's at the other side. Don't you remember the black look of it on the hillside, off the Melton and Oakham road?"

All were hurrying across the rough bottom, with its hillocks and furze bushes, and patches of withered bracken; then, gathering in the narrow bit that let them in under a fringe of trees, mounting upwards. On the farther side of the summit they came out above a thick plantation; and there they drew rein and waited, unsheltered, bare to the sky overhead.

Down came the rain.

"I wish I was dead," said a lank man behind Kilgour. "I wish I was fighting a bye-election!"

Those who were near huddled into the bristling hedge that might break an east wind, but was useless against this downpour. A few slunk back over the brow, and herded under the trees; the rest sat stubbornly on their horses, humping their shoulders, their dripping faces set grimly towards the cover below; hearkening to hounds.

"Would you rather be pelted with words?" said Kilgour, ramming his hat over his nose.—"Surely they trickle off you.... Jerusalem! we'll be drowned."

The lank man turned up his collar, feeling for a button.

"Well, they are dry!" he said.

"They don't give you rheumatism, I grant you," said a fat man beside him; "but they aren't healthy. I don't care what a man's trade is, if he can discourse about it, it's improbable he can do his job. And yet we poor devils of politicians have to spin our brains into jaw— —"

"True," said Kilgour. "You don't trust a glib fellow to dig your garden.... And yet you turn over your country to him."

The fat man grunted.

"*I* never want to open my mouth again," he said. "I'm addressing six meetings a week in my constituency, and nothing will go down with 'em but ranting. Tell you what, Kilgour, we're going on wrong principles altogether. What we want is Government by Minority. Just you get on a platform and look down on their silly faces—! The fools are in the majority in any walk of life; they swamp the sensible chaps, even Solomon noticed that. And it's the fools we must please, because they are many. We take their opinion; we let them settle things. The whole system is upside down."

"There's something in that," said Kilgour. "It always amuses me how you vote-catchers despise a man who works with his head; and bow down to your ignorant fetish the working man."

There was a slight disturbance in the cover, but nothing came of it. People shifted backwards and forwards; there was a smell of wet leather and steaming horses.

"Are you cold?" said Barnaby.

Susan smiled. He was between her and the worst of it; the rain beat on his upturned face as he sheltered her. She liked watching him ... she was not unhappy.

The lank man was trying to light a cigar. He glanced up between his hollowed fingers, his eyes twinkling in a creased red face.

"Our lives aren't worth living, Mrs. Barnaby," he said. "We are all made so painfully aware of our inferior status. The tail wagging the dog; that's what we have come to."

The fat man followed his glance, and his disgusted expression gave way to a friendly gleam. His puffy eyelids quivered.

"Let us grumble," he said. "You see how the weather behaves to us when we escape for a week-end from bondage. There isn't a bright spot anywhere but one tale I heard lately in my division."

The lank man tossed away his match; the cigar was drawing.

"And what was that?" he said.

"Well, it seems they got a Cabinet Minister down to rant against me," said the fat man, chuckling. "He had made himself particularly obnoxious to our militant sisters, and there were terrible hints as to what the ladies were going to do about him. So a London paper commissioned their blandest reporter to call on 'em, and incidentally get at their intentions;—and he stuck a flower in his buttonhole and tackled an engaging young suffragette, who confided in him the tremendous secret. Swore him, of course, to silence——"

"And the wretch betrayed her?"

The politician grinned.

"They were going to disguise themselves as men," he explained, "and pervade the meeting in the likeness of divers of my rival's most prominent supporters. *She* was to make up as a well-known farmer who happened to have lumbago;—leggin's, and corporation, and side-whiskers gummed on tight."

"Pity she let it out," said Kilgour.

"Aha!" said the other man, "she was artless. Well the news got down to 'em somehow, just in time for the meeting, and they set a bodyguard over anybody who looked suspicious. Couldn't keep out their principal backers, or insult 'em by explaining, and hadn't time to investigate.—And my rival got on his legs.—I'm told they were all more or less in hysterics, each man glaring at his neighbour. And these whiskers looked jolly unnatural in the artificial light. My rival had got as far as to mention his 'right honourable friend who, at great inconvenience'—when that old farmer started to blow his nose. 'Turn her out!' he screeched, and four men seized the astonished old chap, and hoisted him, kicking and bellowing, to the door.... There was a glorious row, I'm told. It practically broke up the meeting."

CHAPTER VI

"Ah," said Kilgour, "politics aren't always an arid waste."

"No, occasionally there is rain in the desert. Are we ever going to move. I'm soaking."

In the dark heavens the clouds were frayed by glimmering streaks of light. Barnaby moved impatiently, and beyond him Julia Kelly passed by, changing her station. The girl who was sheltered by his shoulder had forgotten that Julia must be there. She felt suddenly that she was a stranger.

How often must he and Julia have hunted together, how often they must have ridden side by side, sharing the day's fortunes; whispering contentedly to each other as he shielded her from the storm!—More telling than speech had been Julia's half-sad, half-reproachful smile.

"They've got him out!" cried Kilgour, spinning round and heading a mad stampede. As the rest imitated him, Barnaby turned to Susan. "I'm not going to let you out of my sight!" he said.

Down the hill they raced. Hounds were flinging themselves across, bursting louder and louder into cry, proclaiming that they were on his line. And now nobody minded rain.

For a little while Susan felt the magic of it again; the swing of the gallop, the exhilaration of the jumps as they came; but all too soon she flagged. They were hunting slower; hounds were not so sure of the scent; they were slackening, losing faith. The huntsman went forward, and the Master stopped the field. Then they went on again, running in a string up the hedge.

Barnaby turned his horse's head and let the crowd go by. He looked at her significantly. How did he know that she could not keep on much longer?

"I'll take you home now," he said.

"Oh, don't!" she cried. "I am so sorry.... Don't let me spoil your day."

He laughed.

"I'll pick them up again later on," he said. "We must do the correct thing, mustn't we? It would look bad if I let you go home alone.—Good heavens, how tired you are! You can hardly sit on your horse."

*****

Lady Henrietta, the mischief-maker, waited with equanimity for Barnaby to come home. He had brought Susan back and gone off again on a fresh horse, giving her no opportunity of a passage-at-arms with him.

When he did return his coolness was disappointing. She waited until she could contain herself no longer.

"Why don't you ask after Susan?" she said at last. He looked up then. His clothes had dried on him, he had changed lazily into slippers, and was warming his shins at the fire. They had finished the day with a clinking run. "She's not ill?" he said.

"I put her to bed," said Lady Henrietta, "when she came in. The poor child could hardly move.... I suppose you bullied her frightfully when she turned up?"

Barnaby went on stirring his tea and stretching himself to the blaze.

"I told her to have a hot bath and a good long rest," he said, in a grandmotherly tone. "What did you expect? Were you hoping that I should beat her?"

"I was hoping all kinds of things," said Lady Henrietta.

"Such as—?"

She lost all patience. What was the use of plotting if nothing she could devise would rouse him? Anything would be more satisfactory than that maddening smile of his.

"Do you want to break the child's heart?" she cried.

For a moment she fancied that he was startled; she could not see his face so well, but the cup clattered in his hand. Then she discovered that he was laughing at her.

"Has Susan complained?" he said.

"She?" said Lady Henrietta. "Oh, how little you understand her! She'll never complain of you. All I hear I have to screw out of other people. From what they tell me—! Oh, *she'll* never complain, though you and your Julia make yourselves a by-word!"

She paused there, confident that there would be an outburst. Her triumphant expectation was dashed; she was nearly struck dumb with astonishment when she heard his voice.

"It's a queer world, mother."

This was indeed serious. He was not even angry;—and she had hoped to make him furious. She scanned him anxiously, stricken with alarm.

"You aren't well?" she said.

"I'm a little bothered," he said. "Look here, mother; supposing—well, supposing a man were horribly, irretrievably, fond of a woman,—and would be a regular cur if he let her know;—would you condemn him for building up a kind of rampart, playing with fire that he knew couldn't burn him, to keep him from losing his head, and hurting the thing he—the thing that was precious to him? Oh, damn it all, you can't possibly understand."

It was plain as a pikestaff. Lady Henrietta was justified of her mischief-making. Something must be done. There was law and order in any tactics that might vex the siren who was still robbing her of her boy. Never in this world would there be peace between her and Julia.

"If," she said, "you want me to believe that you married Susan to stick her up like a ninepin between you and a woman who threw you over, who can't bear us to imagine you are consoled— —!"

She broke off indignantly, but Barnaby would not quarrel. He got up and laid his hand caressingly on her shoulder.

"Don't excite yourself, mother," he said. "I was talking nonsense. So are you.... If I were you I wouldn't meddle. It's more dangerous than you know."

Then he went away to change out of his hunting clothes, and she watched his departure with a wistful exasperation, lying back on her sofa.

"What a nuisance a heart is!" she said to herself. "He would have had it out with me but for that."

CHAPTER VII

Susan was in the garden.

There had been a frost in the night, and the bushes crackled; the late winter sun was thawing it in the branches. Behind the cloudy glass in the greenhouses were primulas and hyacinths, and all manner of scented things, a bright blur against the panes; but she walked rather the slippery paths in the lifeless garden.

She tried to picture the blackened tufts tall spikes of blossom, and the long line of rose trees, all muffled in dried fern, a bewildering lane of sweetness. Imagination failed her. The blackbird that shot out of the yew tree, screaming his sharp, sweet call; the little wagtail running at a wise distance in the path behind;—they might guess and remember what they would find in spring. She would be gone then; she would have stepped off the stage.

Foolishly she counted up the memories she would carry with her, looked back at the great old house, so warm inside. Strange to think of the time, so impossibly near, when Barnaby would release her, would tell her that he had made his arrangements for her to slip out of this fantastic life without scandal.

Well, she had played up to him; she had never lifted a miserable face, imploring him not to make her suffer so.

Something was choking in her throat. She had not realized how utterly she must pass out of his life until it struck her that she would never see one of these English flowers. The garden became unbearable, taunting her with its unknown mysteries, its hidden promise; and she hurried down the weather-stained wooden steps into the park.

There were rabbit tracks in the grass, and live things rustled in the spinney. A mat of beech-leaves kept the primroses warm. She leant wistfully over the rail, gazing down from the slatted bridge at the water. It was rushing past, very deep.

And then she found a snowdrop....

She heard the dogs scampering and looked up.

"There you are," said Barnaby, putting his arm through hers in friendly fashion. "—The servants, you know!" he reminded her in parenthesis, jerking his head towards the distant windows. "Let's gratify 'em, poor souls. They'll like to see us arm in arm."

He threw a stick to the dogs, and they scurried down the bank to retrieve it, but, missing it, found distraction in rummaging for a water rat. Then he turned again to Susan. She had plucked the snowdrop. That at least was given to her....

CHAPTER VII

"You looked like that flower," he said, unexpectedly, "when I saw you first."

She answered him valiantly.

"Was I so pale with fright?"

"I wasn't thinking of that," he said; "but—the thing hasn't been so difficult, has it, after all? I didn't ask too much of you? We have been good comrades and all that, haven't we, Susan? You have never wished— —?"

Wished it undone? She could not speak. It was over. He was going to tell her that it was over. She thought of that far-off night of amazement, of her panic-stricken impulse, of his hand on her shoulder that had stopped her flight.... Ah, it had been worth it all. Passionately she was glad of it. She had had so much.

"No," she said, "I have never wished— —" and, like him, she left the words unfinished.

And then, with the past close upon her, she forgot everything but him. How she used to think of him, dream of him, dead, who had come to her rescue!

"Oh!" she cried softly, touching his rough tweed sleeve, "isn't it wonderful that you are alive!"

They stood a minute or two in silence, neither speaking, and then Barnaby broke the spell.

"Why did you wander down here in all that drenching grass?" he said. "Your feet are wet."

She began to laugh, helplessly, and almost against her will.

"How like a man!" she said. "You all think it the direst calamity that can happen. You remind me of Vernon Whitford, who, when the poor heroine was despairing, was principally troubled because her boots were damp."

"I know," said Barnaby. "That's my mother's beloved book. She got me to read it too. Some of it stumped me, but I remember that much. How did it go?" his voice dropped. "'He clasped the visionary little feet, to warm them on his breast.'"

It hurt her to feel her cheek burning scarlet. There was no reason. She hurried to defend herself from the wild fancies that might fill a dangerous pause.

"If," she said, and it was anger at herself that made her voice unsteady, "I had thrown myself over this bridge into the river, you would have cried out indignantly—'She'll catch cold!'"

"I might," he said gravely. "We are material wretches. You must come back with me and change your stockings."

He marched her towards the house. One startled, serious look he gave her, but his voice maintained the determined lightness with which it was necessary to face the realities of their bargain. The funny side of it was the only side that would bear looking at.

"You're not impatient?" he said. "You like the hunting? and the life over here? Can you stand it a little longer? We'll clear as soon as we decently can, and think out the tragedy that shall part us."

"Yes," she said; she was a little breathless. The windows yonder were winking flame; it looked as if the house was on fire, but it was only the setting sun....

"There's that horse my mother presented to you," he went on. "You will have to keep him as a souvenir. Hang him round your neck in a locket, what?"

She could but laugh at his whimsical suggestion.

"I'll keep nothing," she said. "An actress doesn't claim the stage properties; her paper crown, her gilt goblet, her royal dresses. Not a poor strolling actress like me, at least. Please, please—" her voice shook a little. He must be made to understand so much, jest and earnest. "Let me go out as you snuff a candle."

"Will you?" he said.

They had nearly reached the house; the glancing windows that had shone afire in their eyes were dark.

"I didn't come out to plan tragedies," said Barnaby. "I was sent to fetch you. The Duchess is in there with my mother. There's the Hunt Ball on in a day or two, and she wants us to dine and go with her party. I think she has some notion of keeping her eye on you. She thinks that I treat you badly."

Susan hung back.

"Must I go?" she said.

"Of course," he said cheerily. "I'd never hear the last of it if I went without you. And my mother is awfully keen on you eclipsing the rest. She's sending in to the bank for all the family trinkets."

"I wonder you are not afraid of my running away with them," she flung at him recklessly.

Barnaby laughed at her as one might at a foolish child.

"Oh," he said. "I'll be there, mounting guard."

*****

The Duchess was lodged in a ramshackle way over a shop. She was not particular. After hiring all the stabling that was to be had in Melton, she had packed herself into a few odd rooms, approached by a dark entry and a narrow stair. It made her feel, she said, like an eagle.

But sometimes her hospitality outdid her accommodation. On the night of the ball she had asked as many people as could be squeezed into her dining-room; all intimate enough not to mind rubbing elbows; and dinner was a scramble.

"The youngest," she proposed, "shall sit with his back to the door, and duck when the plates are handed in over his head.... Do be careful. I put a little man there last year, but when the door opened he used to chuck up his head like a horse, and smashed no end of china."

Having settled this, she threw up a window and rang a bell violently up and down.

"That is for dinner," she said. "It has to be cooked outside, and my people dawdle so. Would you believe it, I was ten minutes ringing for my maid when I came in from hunting. She lodges a few doors higher up, and I had quite a crowd in the street."

"I remember," said Kilgour, "last time I dined with you, one or two bets were laid as to what was happening to the soup in the street below."

"Accidents do happen," she acknowledged. "It isn't quite true, however, that I stuck out my head once and caught them scooping up the sauce."

Susan, wedged in a corner between Kilgour and another equally massive person, was puzzled by the face of a woman opposite, who was smiling at her.

"Don't you know me?" said she. "I recognized you by the dress you have on. I am Mélisande."

She noticed the girl's bewildered look at her yellow hair.

"I keep a black transformation for the shop," she said. "My own idea. But didn't you know my nose? How dear of you to forget it. People call it my trade mark, and say it's Jewish. The worst is, I haven't really shut up shop. I have a young hedgehog to chaperon here to-night. Oh, I am perfectly unashamed!—She is all prickles, but worth a great deal of money. I really couldn't bring her down with me, so she is coming by herself in a special train, or some such extravagance. I thought she might do for Rackham."

"What?" said Barnaby. "Aren't you rather hard on my cousin?"

"It is because he is your cousin," said Mélisande, "I am offering him the hedgehog. Have you ever considered what your reappearance meant to him? Don't we all know how hard up he is, and what a boon your inheritance would have been? If I don't step in with my benefaction he'll possibly murder you."

"Scarcely!" said Barnaby.

"Let me see," said Mélisande. "Give me your hand."

But he would not.

"You will frighten my wife," he said.

"Give me the glass he was drinking out of," said Mélisande. Barnaby's neighbour pushed it over to her, and she peered into it with alarming gravity. Silence waited on her prediction. She raised the glass, swung it round thrice, and spilt a little water.

"I've thrown out a misfortune," she said. "A terrible misfortune," and looked round for applause.

"I am eternally obliged to you," said Barnaby. "Thanks!" But she would not give up his glass.

"There are strange things here," she said, clasping her hands, and gazing into it with half-shut eyes. Barnaby reached over and captured the glass.

"We don't want her to reveal all our secrets, do we, Susan?" he said, and saved the situation by drinking the secrets down.

His presence of mind turned the laugh against Mélisande, whose expression was a study. Ignoring public ridicule, she affected to meditate on his disturbing action.

"I wish I could remember what that portends," she said solemnly. "I rather think it was fatal."

But Barnaby refused to be overawed. He was in a mood of tearing gaiety that Susan did not quite understand. She herself, although she knew that it was absurd, had had a superstitious fear of that glass of water....

"Let's go on to the ball," said the Duchess.

In the general confusion the girl found herself on the stairs with Mélisande, still ruffled. Somehow their glances met.

"Barnaby would turn anything into a joke. He was always like that," said she. "He hasn't any sense of decorum."

"—And you witches," remarked Kilgour, who was close behind, "haven't a sense of humour."

The sorceress pursed her lips.

"Was there anything—bad?" asked Susan.

She was ashamed of the foolish impulse that made her ask. Mélisande looked at her indulgently. But her disclaimer was too hasty to be convincing. In a way, it was more disquieting than if she had overwhelmed the sinner's wife with evil prognostications.

"There was nothing in it. Nothing!" she said, but her voice lacked conviction.

"That's right. Don't frighten us," said Kilgour.

Susan was not frightened. But she could not shake off an unaccountable nervousness;—could not forget Mélisande's wild sayings.... Why was she afraid of Rackham?

It was odd that as soon as they came into the ballroom her eyes should light on him. Everybody was arriving at once, jammed in under the gallery;—and Rackham was pushing through the crowd to her side, and she could not fly.

"What is the matter?" said Barnaby. "Why, you're trembling?"

The truth came out before she could stop herself, though she could not explain it.

"I am shy," she said. "—And I don't want to dance with your cousin."

He did not scoff at her. He took her programme and scribbled his name across it.

"See," he said. "Whatever he asks you for, say you're dancing it with me. How will that do? Fill it in with any of the others, of course, just as you like; and let me know what I am booked for later."

CHAPTER VII

He moved on in the swaying throng, distracted by somebody signalling to him, hailed on all sides, nodding to his friends. Other men were surrounding Susan. She could smile at them now, although Rackham was at her side.

"They're just finishing number one," he said. "Will you give me number two?"

"I am dancing it with my husband."

"Number three, then?"

"I am dancing it with my husband."

Another claimed her attention; she gave him a dance quickly. Kilgour, who could not get near her, held up five fingers to her above the bobbing heads in the crowd. She counted them gaily, putting down the number.

Rackham was still at her side, insisting, but her answer was the same. He looked at her queerly.

"You seem to be dancing everything, more or less, with your husband."

Kitty Drake, floating in like a smoke wreath, put in her word.

"A husband," she said sapiently, "is the only possible partner for a frock like hers. *I* always come to the Melton Ball in rags."

But when Rackham had departed, she looked curiously at Susan.

"You were rude to him," she whispered. "Was it the frock, or what? I am safe."

"I don't know," said Susan. "It is very unreasonable of me, but—I am always a little frightened when he is near me."

Kitty seemed to think that she understood.

"Reason?" she said. "My good girl, I've known more women wrecked because they were ashamed to give in to their frightened instincts than I dare remember. Don't begin to reason! It's simply a machine for making mistakes; it never mends them. Go and be happy. Go and dance with your husband!"

Barnaby had come to her, and there was pity as well as liking in Kitty's little push.

"Shall we begin?" he said, and his arm went round her as she swung out with him on to the shining floor. Dimly she was aware of music, of lights and people; an atmosphere of enchantment.

"Tired?" he said, pausing.

"Tired? Oh, no," she panted, as if he had asked her the strangest question.

"I didn't know you could ride," he said, "and I didn't know you danced. I really know very little about you, Susan."

They had stopped a minute near a ring of idlers who had drifted on to the floor, and somebody caught up his words.

"Have you never danced with her before, Barnaby?"

"No," he said, and bent to gather her train himself, that the weight of it should not tire her arm.

"Do you hear that?" chuckled the man behind them. "Never rode with her, never danced with her. What on earth did he find to do?"

"Made love to her, of course."

Susan felt his arm tighten round her as they whirled into the dizzy spaces.

"I've never made love to you, have I, Susan?"

He was breathing quicker; her cheek almost touched his as he bent his head; her pulses were beating in tune with his. In a sudden faintness she shut her eyes.

And then the music crashed into silence and she was leaning against a pillar, stupidly watching the brilliant scene. There was a great buzz of talking under the gallery, and Barnaby was turning to his friends. She heard his voice now and then amidst the babel, but it was Kilgour and Gregory Drake who were trying to amuse her, picking out the celebrities, good and wicked, in that assembly of glittering dresses and scarlet coats.

"You'll notice," Kilgour was saying, "it's the older men who are dancing, and the young 'uns are looking on. They've no stamina, the lads! Do you see that woman like a tub, with hungry eyes?—She was a beauty once, but when her admirers began to slink off she went in for spirits—that awfully unpleasant kind that you can't absorb. She's always calling 'em up and setting 'em on to tell tales about her dearest friends."

"Yes," said Gregory, "it's really more unhealthy to offend her now than when she was an anarchist and used to spring little clicking machines on you and offered to explain how they worked. She got into hot water once, while it lasted, making herself a side-show at a bazaar. Some foreign personage was attending, and a rumour started that she meant to wind up her clock in earnest. It emptied the hall like winking. The Board of Charitables were no end annoyed."

"They say her fellow anarchists begged her to take her name off their books. Said she brought 'em into contempt."

"That wasn't why," said Gregory. "It was because she would bring Toby, her mastiff, to all their meetings. He and Biff, the thing she carried in her muff, used to scare 'em out of their lives."

"Look at that shop window!" said Kilgour, as another woman, smothered in diamonds, canted past.

"American, isn't she?—Cummerbatch married her for her money, and of course they're wretched. It never pays——"

Susan was conscious that the speaker had checked himself, in his face a ludicrous awkwardness. Had the world jumped to a similar conclusion about her and Barnaby? Instinctively she turned her head. She wanted to share the joke with him, to see his delighted appreciation;—but he was not near.

And he did not dance with her any more. The night dragged on, and one man after another bent his sleek head and offered her his arm. All Barnaby's friends were rallying to her flag. Still, in its turn, would come a star in her card, a dance that found her waiting for a partner who did not come.

After one of these blanks she came face to face with him in the Lancers. He was romping as violently as the rest, charging down the room;—and as the chain of dancers burst it was his arm that kept her from falling into a bank of pale tulips against the wall.

"Wasn't the last dance ours?" he said. "I'm awfully sorry:—but you are getting on all right, aren't you? Plenty of substitutes? I've been watching them buzzing round you."

She smiled at him bravely. How like life this dancing was ... meeting and parting, and strange companions.... For the first and last time she was linking arms with Julia.

Later on she saw Rackham on his way to her. It was almost the first time that evening that she was unsurrounded. She had felt him watching her; awaiting his time to swoop. Barnaby had not been visible during the last two dances, and this, alas! was one that was glorified with a star.

"Yes," said Rackham, before she could speak, "I know;—you are dancing it with your husband."

There was no anger in his voice; only a kind of sardonic amusement, as if he could afford to forgive her for that rebuff. She looked vainly for Barnaby.

"As a matter of fact," said Rackham coolly, "he has delegated his privilege to me."

"I am tired," she said. It was true; very tired and forsaken.

"Then we'll sit it out," said Rackham, no whit abashed. He carried his point over her weariness; she wondered dully why she had been afraid of him, and she was too sad to struggle. She let him take her up the stairs into the far corner of the gallery, now deserted, and sat with her arms on the rail, gazing absently on the flitting brightness that mocked her wistful mood below.

All at once she started. Her wandering thoughts were fixed.

"What are you saying to me?" she cried.

Rackham was very near her, his head bent, his voice low and passionate in her ears.

"What I have always wanted to say to you," he said. "You guessed it, didn't you? You were a little afraid of me;—just a little. You've been trying to put it off.... But don't you remember the first time we met—and that afternoon down by the spinney, when I told you I was your friend?"

She began to shiver. His hand, shutting the idle fan, was imprisoning hers as it clenched itself on her knee.

"I was not listening to you!" she cried desperately. "I was not thinking of you. How dare you?"

"What were you thinking of then?" said Rackham. "Not of Barnaby, who has gone back to his first love and forgotten that you exist."

"He sent you to me," she said piteously.

"Oh, that was a lie," said Rackham. "He didn't even trouble as much as that."

She had sprung to her feet and her face was as white as ashes. For how long had this man been telling her that he loved her? She had been deaf to him, had caught his words without understanding their import, murmuring "Yes" to him, while her eyes and her heart were searching for one figure to pass in the dizzy scene below.

"You are mad," she said.

"Mad if you like," said Rackham. "After all, I am Barnaby's cousin, and it's probably in our blood. Look at him, still crazed over a woman who jilted him years ago!"

She flung up her head, compelled by a piteous instinct to play her part.

"And I am Barnaby's wife," she said bravely.

He looked at her fixedly, making no motion to let her pass him.

"Are you?" he said.

The band seemed to burst into clamour and die away; but they were all dancing; there must be music still, although she could not hear anything but these two syllables. She kept her eyes steady. Perhaps he did not grasp the significance of his words.

"You have insulted me enough," she said to him slowly.

A wild eagerness lighted his face.

"I'm not insulting you," he said. "I leave that to him.... I'm asking you to be my wife, Susan. Let him go. Let him release himself. Leave him to the woman from whom you can't keep him.—Come away with me,—and marry me!"

"I—cannot," she said.

He had to fall back then and let her go. But he followed her down the stairs. The light in his eyes flickered out, leaving a sullen admiration.

"Well," he said, "I warn you. I've a bit of a score to settle with Barnaby."

She turned on him. She had reached the bottom; her foot was on the crimson carpet that lay under the gallery; a little way off a handful of men were talking with their backs turned, hilarious at the climax of a sporting tale. She looked at the dark face above her; her lips were white now, her eyes were blazing. "Are you threatening—him?" she cried, and the devil in Rackham smiled.

She took a few rash steps, hardly knowing in what direction.

"You needn't look for him here," said Rackham bitterly. "Don't let his friends think you jealous."

From where she stood she could see in at the open doorway of one of the sitting-out rooms, a dim, mysterious haunt of palms, the chairs drawn back in the shadow. Was not that Barnaby and a woman in a glittering green dress, listening with her face uplifted—?

Ah, what right had she to run to him?—One of the men standing about under the gallery had looked round. She heard him mutter it was a shame. What was a shame? Not anything that could be spoken or done to her.... She threw up her head, walking straight on as if she were walking in her sleep. The Duchess and Kitty Drake were together half-way up the room; they moved down to meet her, exchanging looks.

"My dear," said the Duchess solemnly, "you look fatigued."

"I am tired," she said.

"I thought so. Fagged out. You have danced too much. Major Willes—"

She called a man to her side and sent him on an immediate errand. When he was gone she returned to Susan.

"I've sent somebody to fetch your husband," she said. "He ought to take more care of you. I shall scold him."

"Oh, don't!" she cried faintly, but her champions took no notice; and soon Barnaby himself came swinging along the room.

"Barnaby," said the Duchess, "you ought to be ashamed of yourself. Take your wife up to supper."

The first rush was over upstairs in the supper-room, and Barnaby found a corner. She sat with him at a little round table behind a tall plant that shut off the world with its wide green fronds, some sheltering exotic. And he was pouring out champagne, a drink she hated. She put her hand over the top of the glass, and he caught it and lifted it off, holding it in his while he poured on unchecked.

"It's not good stuff,—but it's good for you. Drink!" he said.

He seemed to be laughing at her from an immeasurable distance; his prescription had made her dizzy.

"It will go off in a minute; you wanted it badly," he was saying, in a voice that sounded far away and unlike his own.

"It has gone to my head," she said, appealing to him. "I'm afraid I shall say something silly. Don't let me. Don't let me talk....'"

"Why not? There is nobody listening," he was saying, encouraging her; amused.

And Susan heard her own voice. Her head was spinning; she was talking against her will.

"Why did you never come back and dance with me?" she was asking. It seemed to her that there was a long pause, and then his answer came, low and close.

"I did not dare," he said.

"Oh," she said piteously;—no, not she, but the imprudent, tired girl whose head was giddy, and who did not know what she said. "Oh,—how funny!"

Perhaps he was throwing dust in people's eyes,—trying to blind them to his fluttering, like a burnt moth, round Julia. If they saw him sitting up here in a corner with her, and she was happy, they would think there was nothing in it. He must be trying to make her laugh. Well, she must help him. She could say something funny too.

"There's a man downstairs," she told him, "who asked me to marry him."

"What?" said Barnaby. He started as if he had been shot.

"He said he loved me," she repeated. "He wished me to go away and release you and marry him."

"Who?"

"You were with the only woman you ever cared for. That was what he said. I had nobody to keep him away from me...."

"Oh, I was with the woman I cared for, was I?" he said. "And who the devil is it wants horsewhipping when I get at him?"

The deadly calm in his voice arrested her. What had she said to him, babbling in her unhappiness? Alarm steadied her; the dizziness was passing.

"I will not tell you," she said, forgetting how vainly she had looked for him to shield her.

His eyes were blue as steel. She had never seen him angry until to-night.

"I'll make you," he said.

They stared at each other a minute, her eyes as unflinching as his were hard. Across the silly little supper table with its glass and silver, its green, gold-tipped bottles, and its tumbled flowers, he leaned and gripped her hands.

"Did you tell him you are not my wife?" he said.

There was a whiff of scent in their neighbourhood; the great green fronds spreading behind him were rudely stirred. A passing couple must have brushed against that screen on their way to the stairs. A burst of merriment came from the upper end of the room. But these two were as much alone as if it had been a desert.

So that was why he was angry. He believed that she had broken faith....

"I told him nothing," she said.

Barnaby took a long breath. She felt his grip relax.

"You are a good girl," he said. "You wouldn't break your promise. I suppose I've no right to order you:—I'll find him out for myself. Tell me one thing, and we'll let it go—"

She waited. There had been something very bitter to her in his relief. All he asked of her was to keep the secret until he was tired of the joke....

"Susan," he said. "Did you want to tell him?"

What did that matter to him? Supposing she had—wanted? Supposing she would have given worlds to exchange her difficult post for one so different, so secure? — Her cheek burned.

"I would sooner have died," she said.

*****

Rackham stood under the gallery in a black mood, watching the Duchess send her messenger to hunt out the missing husband. He saw Julia, bereft of her cavalier, pausing uncertainly; and a satiric impulse moved him to join her.

"Come and have supper with me," he said.

"I am engaged to Barnaby," she said, a little defiantly.

"They've sent him up with his wife," he retorted, and his mocking tone seemed to please her. She submitted and pressed his arm.

"Poor Barnaby!" she said. "It's an awful muddle."

She was looking very lovely and pathetic. The man who had once been entangled a little way in her toils himself and, having failed to succumb, was naturally inclined to despise her, admired her pose. It was hardly to be wondered at if Barnaby, who had been mad about her once, should be incapable of resisting the allurement of these dark eyes, so deep and so reproachful. He could not help speculating how far she was in earnest, and how far a hurt vanity inspired her. Curiosity piqued him.

"I understand," he said gravely, as they passed out and began to climb to the supper-room. It amused him to feel that her confidential attitude, her claim on his sympathy, was a subtle intimation that he had been the unlucky cause of the fatal misunderstanding, and must therefore be kind to her. All at once he had a perverse inclination to cast himself in the scale again. Why not? It would be a bitter joke on Barnaby, and it suited his savage humour.

"I like your dress," he said. His change of tone surprised her. She glanced at him swiftly, half-turning as she mounted, her green garments rippling as she lifted her train on one smooth arm, displaying a whirl of skirts and one little green sequin slipper. "Ah," she said, "down below they've been reviling me for a mermaid, and complaining bitterly of my tail."

"And so," said Rackham, "the little slipper is betrayed, to dispel the illusion?"

"Perhaps," said Julia. She used, at one time, to smile up in his face like that.... A vindictive sense of his power possessed him, flattering him on this night of defeat. In his heart he was still fiercely worshipping the pale girl who had flouted him, clinging obstinately — Oh, she was a fool, and so was Barnaby; — and the irony of it was that he had only to lift his finger — !

"We'll find a place by ourselves," he said, confidentially, passing into the room. Inside it he took a step or two, glancing about him. There were vacant seats on the right, but the tables had a battered air. Farther down, perhaps — ; yes, farther down, near the wall. He turned back to look for his partner, and the sight of her face amazed him. With a promptitude that surprised himself he pulled her back, and got her outside the room. Was it possible that he had been mistaken in her, or could a woman push affectation as far as that?

She broke into a kind of gasping exclamation that was not intelligible at first, and he stared at her in limitless amazement.

"Oh, poor Barnaby, oh, poor Barnaby!" she repeated. There was a ring of triumph in her incoherent voice. She had gone mad, he fancied.

"Hush!" he said. "They'll hear you."

He was glad he had shut that door, and thankful there was not a soul on the stairs.

"I was right!" she said, "I was right.... I knew it! You were there when she came here first as his widow, and I told his mother to her face it was a wicked plot!"

"Julia," said Rackham, "you don't know what you are saying."

She controlled herself a little. He held her wrist.

"Didn't you see them in there?" she asked. "Didn't you hear him?"

"If you mean Barnaby," he said, "I was looking out for our places. I didn't notice whereabouts they were till you clutched at me. They didn't see us at all."

"I heard him," she said, in the same wild key of triumph. "I heard his own words.—He said she was not his wife."

"Hush!" said Rackham vehemently, and then, more slowly—"Julia, are you sure of that?"

She tried to imitate him, to whisper, but she was too excited.

"Sure!" she said, laughing hysterically. "I know his voice so well. There was a green plant between us——"

"Wait," said Rackham. "There's somebody coming. We'll go down. Damn! there are people everywhere—! Get a shawl, and we'll go out into the street."

Julia resisted him.

"Why are you dragging me away?" she rebelled. "You can't keep me quiet. Think how I've been treated! I could scream it to all the world!"

A woman could not have silenced her, but her emotional nature yielded finally to the rough coaxing of a man. He almost swung her downstairs into the draughty passage and, raiding the ladies' cloakroom, snatched up the first wrap that lay to his hand.

A chill wind blew up the steps, but there was still a persistent crew of gazers loitering in the street below. Rackham led her past, and they strolled a little way into the darkness, lighted at intervals by a twinkling lamp. There was no danger there of her making scenes.

"Now," he said. "Now, Julia—!"

"They shall all hear the truth!" she cried. She hung on his arm, gesticulating.

"You wouldn't betray him?" said Rackham, sounding her.

"Him?" she said. "Poor Barnaby! He and I are the victims. Don't you understand yet? When she thought he was dead his mother—just to crush me, just to humble me in the dust!—hired this creature. Don't you remember how she sprung her on us? Who had heard of a marriage? Oh, it was a judgment on her when he came home!"

"She'd hardly look at the case in that light," he said. But Julia was impervious to irony.

"He should have considered me first," she said. "Why do men always sacrifice the one they love best? It's a kind of cruel unselfishness. I was his dearest, a part of himself, and so—and so I'm to bear this trial—! But he might have trusted *me*!"

She was either laughing or sobbing, he was not sure which; the cloak that muffled her hid her face; but her voice raged on, half furious, half triumphant.

"Of course, she's blackmailing him," she said. "That wretch has got him in the hollow of her hand! If he disowned her it would all come out, and it would disgrace his mother. He was always quixotic. And so he is temporizing till he can bribe her to disappear. But Lady Henrietta has no claim on my forbearance!"

She had to pause for breath, and he managed to get in his word.

"I am going to advise you," he said, "to keep quiet over this."

They had come to the end of the street, and were walking back. A dazzle of lights in the distance marked the Corn Exchange. A motor whirred past, its lamps sending a brief glare that was like a searchlight. Already a few were leaving.

"Why?" she said, staring at him.

"You'll be a fool if you talk," he said. "If Barnaby is holding his tongue for his mother's sake, is it likely he'll give way? And you have no proofs. Whatever you say, he'll deny it. He mightn't forgive you, either. Be sensible.... Wait a bit, and I'll make inquiries."

It struck her then as odd that he had accepted her words himself, without argument, with no incredulous opposition, such as she was beginning to realize must fall to her lot if she published her tale abroad.

"Did you know from the first?" she cried.

"No," said Rackham, "I didn't know. But I guessed."

They had nearly reached the steps, and he slackened, regarding her narrowly; but already she was subdued. It was characteristic of her that she had never seen his admiration for the impostor. Vast as her imagination was, it was blinded by centring on herself.

"And you'll help me? You are on my side?" she said.

He knew then that he had prevailed.

"As long as you are wise," he said. They went up the steps together.

"I had better find my party," she said hurriedly. "I want to go home. Poor Barnaby!—I can't bear to meet him. I am too agitated."

Rackham took back the borrowed cloak and strolled along the passage, in no hurry to return to the ballroom. People were passing in and out; some of them were saying good-night, and one pair were wrangling on their way to the door.

"Who was the man you were flirting with in the street?" said the lover in an angry stutter. The lady scoffed.

"What a story!"

"My brother saw you go out. He came up and chaffed me."

"Your brother is a donkey. It must have been someone else."

"I tell you he recognized you by that chiffon fal-lal you wear!"

Rackham stood on one side. Let them fight it out.... Then his mouth hardened. What was he going to do? He had managed to prevent Julia from spoiling it all, and as long as he could keep her quiet the cards were in his hands.

CHAPTER VIII

"I won't let you go home," said the Duchess. "Barnaby can do as he likes, but you're too tired to mind sleeping in a cupboard."

She held Susan firmly by the arm as she spoke; she had motives. Barnaby deserved to be punished; his conduct with Julia had really been scandalous. But a worn-out girl, a wisp of white satin, was no match for a naughty husband. She would burst into tears and forgive him. Let Barnaby go home by himself, feeling guilty, and brood upon his unkindness. *She* would tell Susan what to do to him in the morning.

With rough kindness she hustled the girl away with her, and having collected her party, ordered them to bed.

"Because," she said, "until some of you are disposed of I can't tell what to do with the others, and I want to know if there are beds enough to go round."

Susan was the first to be bundled into her attic, and lay wearily listening to a far-off commotion. When at last the household had settled down there was a fresh disturbance, and the elder of the two foreign maids mounted, carrying an armful of pillows.

The Duchess herself followed, to excuse the indicated invasion. She was already in her dressing-gown. The maid set up a chair bed that had stood, doubled up, in the corner, and was sent out of the room for a minute.

"I've come to apologize," said the Duchess, "for pitchforking a stranger into your room like this; but I'm sorry for the woman. You are the only one of them I can depend on not to be horrid to her."

She looked round, measuring the space that was to be shared. "I hope," she said, "you won't bump into each other. The truth is, I have a shocking custom of sticking my head out of the window when something is going on outside; and just as I was getting into bed I heard a tremendous buzzing. Everybody must have started. If this was somebody's motor gone wrong, I supposed I ought to offer my hospitality. And it was. The chauffeur was grovelling; a man I knew was storming at him; and a woman wringing her hands on the pavement. I knew her too, perfectly, and she had no business in that man's car."

She stopped to listen.

"I am not," she said, "a universal mender. If people I don't particularly care about are jumping out of frying-pans, I don't preach at them eternal fire. But this fool of a woman had chosen to bolt under my very nose. Providence had cast her upon my doorstep. So I took the hint. Not being a heathen I really had to."

The confidential maid was ascending with someone strange to the place, who stumbled and chattered in halting French.

"I poked my head farther out," said the Duchess, "and shouted—'Is that you, Lady Cummerbatch? Have you had a breakdown?' and it was worth it to see her jump. I don't in the least know what she answered; it sounded hysterical. 'Well,' I said, 'leave your husband to tinker up the machine; it will probably take him hours. I can put you up.'"

"Her husband?" said Susan, puzzled.

"Tact, my child, tact! I sent Fifine down to fetch her, and kept my eye on him. She followed Fifine into the house like a lamb."

She wrapped her dressing-gown closer round her, and prepared to depart.

"I couldn't keep her in my room," she said; "I've two girls camping on the floor. Besides, she would begin confessing everything, and I am certain that I should smack her. Pretend that you are asleep. If she cries, don't notice. Good night, my child."

She patted Susan on the head, looking as if she would have kissed her, but not being accustomed to caresses, did not quite know how.

Then she wheeled round to receive the late visitor, holding up her finger, and crying—"Hush!" very loud.

Susan lay with her face turned from the light and her eyes shut, as she had been bidden. She heard Fifine, after some careful whispering, close the door and make her way down; she heard a smothered sobbing from the improvised bed that almost blocked the chamber;—and then she heard a stealthy noise in the room, and opened her eyes. On the wall she could see the shadow of a person struggling into her clothes, and evidently about to fly. Some instinct made the girl spring up and fling herself against the door.

"Oh! Oh!" said the strange woman, tottering. "Let me out!"

Susan looked her in the face.

"If you want to go," she said, "I will call the Duchess."

The stranger began to cry. She was thin and fair, with a faded skin and unhappy eyes, outstared by a blaze of jewels. Susan remembered seeing her at the ball. Kilgour had called her the Shop Window.

"He's waiting for me. I must go with him," she cried, worked up to a pitch of agitation that deprived her of self-control.

"You shall not," the girl said.

They both heard an engine vibrating far down below. The woman flew to the window. And then the Duchess's strident voice struck into the night from her own window underneath.

"So glad the motor is working. Don't trouble about your wife, Sir Richard.

CHAPTER VIII

She's safely tucked up in bed."

Then a furious backing and grinding, as the car started and rushed away into the darkness, baulked of a passenger.

Susan retired sedately into bed, since it was no longer necessary to guard the door. The woman began to strip off her jewels, that she had put on again, anyhow,—flinging them in a heap on the table.

"Absurd, isn't it?" she said, in a high, unnatural key, "wearing all these.... but I wasn't going to leave them behind."

The girl said nothing; she was embarrassed.

"The Duchess took him for Dicky," the prisoner rambled on. Perhaps she was afraid of silence. "*You* guessed the truth. I saw you at the ball to-night. They were all talking about you, and I liked your diamonds. Did *your* husband marry you for your money?"

Susan drew a sharp breath. Ah, this woman was more to be pitied than she, who had brought sorrow upon herself.

"Oh, you poor thing!" she said softly, sitting up in bed and clasping her hands round her knees.

Lady Cummerbatch was one of those lucky women who find solace in lamentation. They are the fortunate ones, whose bitterness of heart can be dissipated in bitter speech.

"I've heard," she went on, too distracted about her own plight to be conscious of the rank impertinence of which she was being guilty. "I've heard all about your husband. He's the wild Barnaby Hill who was jilted by an Irishwoman and disappeared and married abroad to vex her, and then turned up after his people thought him dead. You're an American too, though you are not my kind. They seem fond of you here; they all take your part;—but what difference does it make? Aren't we two miserable women?"

She began to weep noisily, and then to shiver. Getting into bed, she pulled her fur cloak over her shoulders, and sat hunched up, staring at the light.

"Do you mind my not putting out the candle?" she said. "I can't bear to lie worrying in the dark. If that auto hadn't stuck, and the Duchess hadn't jumped me when I got out to see what was the matter, I'd have been out of my misery.... I said to Sir Richard once—'You married me for my money,' and he laughed in my face and said—'My good young woman, you had an equivalent—you married me for my title.' And then I just screamed, 'I married you for your title! Oh, yes, I married you for your title!' till he banged himself out of the house."

"But if that was not true——" said Susan.

"True? It was all true," she sobbed. "The pity was it didn't keep true. When I married that man I couldn't have told you if his eyes were grey or green. But there—! It wears off with them and it wears on with us."

In her lamentation she continued to identify herself with her compatriot; their common misfortune, as she conceived it, was mixed up in her bewailing.

"Why don't you try it, like me?" she said. "Why don't you run away from him? If you cry and stamp and bluster it makes them vain, but when they've lost you outright they miss you.... Oh, it's awful to live with a man and watch him getting impatient because you are in his way and he's tied to you;—to see him looking hard at you, thinking how could he have paid the price! He tried to be civil at first, but his face soon taught me.... I wonder how long were you deceived?"

"I was never deceived," said Susan, hardly knowing she had uttered that sigh aloud. Her arms were round the other woman now; a poor wretch who had once been happy. Ah, with what pain would she not have gladly purchased some mirage of happiness, some illusion that she was his ... and beloved ... for half an hour!

The haggard butterfly who had been cursed with riches dropped her voice from its wailing tune to a whisper.

"I'm going to France to-morrow," she said. "He won't like that. It will be the same as striking him in the face. He to turn from me to other women who had no money to give him—! When a man sees that what he has tossed in the gutter is precious to another man, when he sees how the other man picks it up,—he feels cheated. It hits him harder than if you had killed yourself. I thought of *that* first. But don't you do it! I knew just how he'd say—'Mad! quite mad!' and bury me and forget me. He'll never lose sight of it if I go away like this—" and her voice rose high—"*that* will let him know how I hate him!"

But when her confidences had tired her out, and she loosed her clasp of Susan, pulling up the quilt and sinking into a wearied slumber,—when the girl lay gazing alone at a light that was burning dim;—there was a cry in the silence.

"I've come back, Dicky! Dicky, let me in—! I've come back."

It was the woman who hated her husband, calling to him in her sleep.

*****

Susan awakened in the morning with music in her ears. Dreaming, she danced with Barnaby, and his arm was round her, his breath quick on her cheek, his face not ... kind.

And as the wild illumination of a dream sometimes teaches what a stumbling consciousness dare not know, so the girl awoke trembling.

But that dream of all dreams was madness.

Into her waking mind came the thought of Rackham, the man who had said he loved her. Had she not always been ill at ease with him, and what was that but a warning instinct, divining, shrinking from the peril in a man's admiration? But Barnaby and she had been such good comrades....

Quaint incidents crowded on her, scenes in the hunting field, Sunday afternoons at the stables,—the day he had cut his finger and she had run to him to bind it up;—the day he had told her the brim of her riding hat was too narrow, and made her try on another that satisfied his inspection.... Oh, they had honourably

CHAPTER VIII

tried not to haunt each other, but all the same.... Dear and safe memories; they blotted out last night.

She raised herself on her elbow and looked across the room at the runaway.

So a woman could sleep whom the casual kindness of an acquaintance had saved from shipwreck; so a woman could sleep who had poured out her soul to a stranger.

Someone was tapping at the door. It was late. Ten, eleven, ah, quite that; and Monsieur had come for Madame and brought her clothes. And Miladi said Madame was to dress in her room, as one was so cramped up here.

The maid waited discreetly at the door, her sharp, foreign eyes taking in everything, the other woman huddled up in bed, her clothes flung all over the floor, her gems scattered recklessly on the table.

Susan slipped on the dressing-gown that had been brought her, and was following, Fifine going down in front as a picket, to see that the coast was clear; when she heard her neighbour calling. Lady Cummerbatch was sitting up in bed.

"I made a fool of myself last night, didn't I?" she said. "Why didn't you smother me with my pillow? Don't be afraid, I'm as wise as an old hen this morning." She pulled the girl close enough to kiss. "You are a dear; you are a dear!" she cried.

Stretching out her arm to the dressing-table, she caught up something from its disordered glitter, squeezing it into Susan's hand.

"Keep it," she said. "I know you've heaps of your own. I saw them last night. But I want you to have something to remember me by. I can do nothing for anybody but give them things.... Do! Please me! I'd have thrown myself out of that window if you hadn't been kind to me."

The girl looked doubtfully at the diamond star that had been thrust upon her.

"If you don't care to wear anything I've worn," said the woman, "put it by. Who knows? Some day you may be glad to have it. If it does come from a worthless creature, it's fit to sell. I've heard of rich women whose husbands ruined them, and who had to pawn their jewels.... How do we know what will happen to you and me?"

Susan went down the irregular flight of stairs. The Duchess was waiting in her room for a word.

"Good morning, my child," she said. "Your husband has very properly come to fetch you. I should advise you to let him off lightly about last night."

The maid had gone out of the room.

"About— —?" faltered Susan.

"Philandering with Julia. I believe in severity, of course," said the Duchess bluntly, "but as a matter of fact Kitty and I have been at him like early birds. Told him what we thought of him, and so forth. Don't look so sorry. It's done him good, and you can descend upon him like a forgiving saint."

"I have nothing to forgive him," the girl protested. "Oh, I wish you would not say that."

The Duchess smiled benevolently at her stammering haste. She fancied she understood.

"I quite forgot," she said, "to ask after that idiot upstairs. *There's* a woman who tried to enrage her husband into paying her more attention by making herself conspicuous with another man. Bad policy, my child. It makes the man think less of her, though it may alarm his possessive instinct;—and, of course, if anybody stole your old coat you'd feel inclined to knock him down:—but that wouldn't make you believe it was as good as new. No, no, it's a fallacious notion. However, we're talking of this person. I'd be sorry for her feelings if I didn't think the shock of being stopped on the brink would bring her to her senses. We are very good-natured among ourselves, but *she* wouldn't find it easy to live it down. She isn't one of us."

She smiled encouragingly at the girl, who was wrapped in her own dressing-gown, a thick masculine garment that sat oddly on her slimness.

"People think," she said, "that we hunting people are a lawless band. They think they can come and do as they like in Melton. Just because we have a sporting sense of loyalty to each other, and stick to our friends when they need us. If you or Barnaby, for example, did anything outrageous, we'd scold you a little and let it drop. But we don't do it with an outsider.... He's brought your habit. Get into your things, my dear."

Barnaby nodded to her cheerfully as she came into the breakfast room. He was sitting on the window seat, and the rest of them were at breakfast. Whether or no they had been attacking him, he did not look cast down.

"Well, how are you?" he said. "Good girl, you are coming hunting. I brought everything, didn't I? They nearly left out your boots."

"Look out and see who that is passing," said the Duchess. Someone was cracking a whip below. He flung up the window, and she came round herself.

"What's the matter?" she said. "Is it a serenade, or do you want some coffee?"

A man with a long nose and a grizzling moustache had halted on his way up the street. Two or three others had left him and were trotting on.

"Have you heard the latest?" he said. "Richard Cummerbatch is drawing all the covers like a raging maniac, roaring for his wife. Her party went back in two cars from the ball last night, and each lot thought she had gone in the other. It appears she's bolted."

"Upon my word," said the Duchess, "if you are going to shout scandal at the top of your voice I shall have to put up my shutters. She is just over your head, Major. She had nowhere to go, since her party went off without her; so I took her in."

"Hey? What?" he said, looking up as quickly as if the lady were a chimney-pot that might fall on him. "—Keep still, horse! You don't say so?"

His face was blank for an instant, but he soon recovered from his disappoint-

CHAPTER VIII

ment. His well of gossip had not run dry.

Cocking his head on one side like a mischievous old bird, he began on another tack.

"Well," he said, "if you're so rough on scandal, you'll have to keep our friend Barnaby in order. What does his poor little American wife say to his goings-on?"

There was an awful pause in the room above.

"Susan," said Barnaby, "he's as deaf as a post. Put your head out and tell him as loud as you can what you think of me."

Somebody began to laugh; the rest followed; and there was no more awkwardness; his presence of mind had saved the situation. As he leaned out of the window with his hand on Susan's shoulder the Major's face was a study. Incontinently he fled.

"There!" said Barnaby, "we have routed the enemy. Let's get on our horses and pursue him. Hullo, who are these? A whole tribe without one sound horse among them."

The Duchess started back.

"Don't tell me it is my friend Wickes," she said. "I promised him weeks ago I'd beat up a little talent for his concert to-night, and I have never done it. For heaven's sake, somebody, volunteer! Is there a woman here who can sing in tune?"

"Do you sing, Susan?" said Barnaby.

"Oh, the man's affectation! Does she or does she not?"

She did not know what impelled her. Perhaps his carelessness; his unshaken attitude of amusement at a position that was—to him—so absurd.

"I could act something, perhaps," she said. The Duchess jumped at her offer.

"Booked!" she declared. "Stop that man clattering past, and tell him I want him to sing *John Peel*. And, Cherry, you'll do for a comic song. You're men, and it doesn't matter about your voices, so long as you wear red coats."

The young man she was ordering pushed away his cup with an injured air. A murmur of—"Delighted, I'm sure. Delighted!" floated up from the street.

"You know I have only one song," he said, "and that is—*The Broken Heart*."

"Well," she said unfeelingly, "you can make it comic."

"Are you coming?" said Barnaby. He was waiting; some of them had already started. The girl caught up her gloves and whip.

"Good-bye, all of you," said the Duchess. "I beg you'll remember your obligations. Barnaby, the thing is at eight. Call down to *John Peel* and tell him.... Whatever you do, don't let my performer come to any harm."

"I will not quit her side for a moment," he promised, and the Duchess shook her head at him as they ran downstairs.

He was laughing as he put her up in the saddle.

"It appears you don't know how to manage a husband," he said. "Don't look so sorrowful. *I* don't mind them.—And the general public is anxious to lend a hand."

They rode soberly side by side, over the noisy cobbles, down to the low white bridge thronged with pedestrians, threading their way amidst the stream that was turning in at the gates farther on to the right.

"We'll keep on, shall we?" said Barnaby. "Hounds will be moving directly, and there'll be a fearful crowd getting out of the Park."

So they held on between the lines of townsfolk and, turning upward, fell in with a cluster of horsemen on the watch, loitering on the hill.

"Awful bore, meeting in the town like this," said one of these peevishly. His horse was eyeing a perambulator strangely, and there was no space for antics. "Why do the Quorn do it?"

"Oh, it pleases the multitude."

There was a roar down below, and a scuffling noise as of hundreds running. Above the bobbing heads passed a glimpse of scarlet, as a whip issued from the green gates, clearing a way for hounds that were hidden from view in the middle of the throng. Barnaby turned his horse round.

"Come on," he said. "We'll wait for them out of the town. I suppose it's the customary pilgrimage? Gartree Hill."

Behind them, louder and louder, drowning the tumult, came the quickening tramp of horses. Their own animals grew excited.

"Sit him tight!" said Barnaby. Her horse had nearly bucked into the last lamp-post at the top of the hill. He would not wait peaceably at the corner, so she took him a few yards farther on, straight over the brow, where the way was not street, but road, looking down upon open country.

"Hullo!" said Barnaby.

The fields that spread underneath were bare and wind-swept; there was no sign of life in them. But what was that brownish dab on the right? Incredulously he watched it travelling up the furrow;—and, convinced, let out a wild yell that made their own horses jump.

"It's a fox!" he said. "It's a fox. Keep your eye on him, Susan, while I fetch them up."

He galloped back, waving his hat to hurry the startled host. The huntsman came swiftly over the hill, and a glance assured him; he touched his horn. In half a minute he and his hounds were scouring over the fields, and the riders who had been at the front were jumping out of the road.

"They've found. They are running!"

The cry was flung from lip to lip along the bewildered ranks that had closed up in expectation of the long jog to cover. A minute more and the crowd had burst like a scattered wave, far and wide.

CHAPTER VIII

Down the slope; up a rise; in and out of a lane defended by straggling blackthorn; dipping over the skyline; the pack was gone. Only the quickest could live with them, only the first away had a chance of keeping up in the run. They were just a handful as they landed over a stake-and-bound into a rolling pasture, a great rough waste where the ridges rose up like billows, crosswise, submerging the horses that were shortening in their stride.

"Good for the liver!" groaned Kilgour, as he rocked up and down. "But what a sell for the crafty ones waiting on Gartree Hill!"

"They'll cut in with us at Great Dalby," said Barnaby, flinging a glance that side. The pack hung to the left, still flying.

"Not much!" said Kilgour. "D'you suppose the fox is stopping with Lydia Measures for a bottle of ginger beer?—What did I tell you? There they go, wide of the village, over the Kirby lane——"

He broke off his ejaculations, pointing triumphantly with his whip, pushing on. A man of his build could not afford to lag behind, unlike those light-weights who could lie by and then come like a whirlwind and make it up. He must keep plodding on. But he took no shame to diverge suddenly to a gate. Let the young 'uns surmount that rasper.

On the high ground above a breathless horde struck in. Rumour, or the wind, or some saving instinct had warned them; they had come at a breakneck pace from their shivering watch elsewhere.

Susan, riding her hardest, with her chin up and rapture on her face, laughed as she heard the frantic thudding of that pursuit.

"They've missed a bit," cried Barnaby at her shoulder. Her horse was faster than his, but was tiring. She was glad to steady him as the pack ran into a strip of trees.

"What a scent!" said Barnaby. "Hark at them! They're sticking to him;—they're driving him up the Pastures!"

He swung round in his saddle, still keeping on. The rearguard, no longer in desperation, were trooping contentedly down the road.

"They'll get left," he said. "They reckon on losing him. Silly asses, they're lighting their cigarettes!"

Slower, but steadily, hounds were running up the wood. Their cry increased in volume, vociferous, echoing in the trees. It sounded a hundred times louder than in the open. And this time there was no changing foxes; they drove him too hard. Out he went at the top, and had no time to twist and turn in again; they were on his heels. Beyond was a steep drop into a village, and then a long struggle, and another drop to a ford. As the last of them were splashing through the water, the first of them were swinging out of their saddles and turning their horses' heads to the wind. They had run to Baggrave, and killed their fox in the Park.

"Three cheers for Barnaby and his outlier," said Kilgour. "That was no poultry-snatcher, but a real beetle-fed warrior. What the dickens shall we do next?"

"Oh, get up in a tree, somebody, like Sister Anne; and rake the horizon for second horses!"

Susan knew that voice. It was Rackham.

"Get up yourself," said Kilgour. "Your history isn't sound. *I* don't trust my weight on anything but a watch-tower."

Susan had turned away her face; she did not want to have to acknowledge Rackham, although he had no shame in approaching her. Nervously she plunged into a rapid argument with Kilgour, whose broad and comfortable presence was a kind of buckler. But through it all she was conscious of him, she heard his voice. He and Barnaby were arranging something about a horse. She did not catch the drift of it, but Rackham turned to her pointedly and asked her opinion.

"I wasn't listening," she said. His glance was penetrating; she could not escape it, and recollection burnt in her cheek. She heard Barnaby whistle suddenly to himself.

Hounds were moving at last, not hurrying, but drifting across the park, searching as they went; and second horsemen were springing up out of nowhere. Those who were lucky were changing horses. Already it was far on in the afternoon.

"That's the worst of beginning so late," said Kilgour. "The day's gone before you know it. And here we've been dawdling, munching.... Now we'll just get away with the twilight after dodging backwards and forwards for an hour or two between the Prince of Wales's and Barkby Holt."

"Shut up, ill prophet!" said Barnaby, as they gathered close in to the cover-side. Already there was a whimper.

But it was late before the prophesied shilly-shallying came to its appointed end, and those who had resisted the false alarms, sticking patiently on guard at a windy corner, saw a fox break at last. A misleading holloa had drawn off the field; they were massing on the other side, out of sight, out of hearing in the rising wind that carried away with it the warning note of the horn. And hounds were slipping out like lightning.

"Come on!" said Barnaby. This time there was no mistake.

It didn't matter that there was a rival shout behind the dense thicket. Let those who liked it exclaim that the pack was divided, and miss a run to hang skirmishing for ever and ever about the Holt.... They had a fox away, and at least half the hounds were on him as he dipped the rise and went spinning into the infinite. Just a handful of riders they were, but high-hearted, as they turned their faces towards the dim red line of the sinking sun.

Miles and miles they seemed to go swinging on. Behind a grey church, round a silent village, and under a rustling wood. The wind was fresh with the breath of twilight; its withering blast died down with that last stinging gust of rain. And hounds were still running as swift as shadows, flickering far and fast.

One by one the rest of them had fallen back; had steadied their faltering horses and listened, beaten. Susan could hardly see the fences as they came up, darker

CHAPTER VIII

and darker against the sky. But her horse rushed at them gallantly, and she had Barnaby to follow. Hounds were invisible now, but near; their cry was fierce behind that clump of trees, impenetrable but for one glimmering gap of light.

"They're running him still!" called Barnaby, plunging in.

His voice was all she wanted. She could not ask more of Heaven than this one gallop; and all her life she would remember that she had ridden it out with him....

They had to ride warily through the trees, feeling their way, trusting in their horses. Here the path was deep and boggy, there water trickled, and the boughs hung low, swishing against them as they went by. Birds whirred restlessly in the creaking branches, and an owl flew shrieking in front of them. When they emerged from that eerie passage everything had grown weird and strange in the cheating dusk.

"That's the horn," said Barnaby. "He's calling them off. Doesn't it sound unearthly?—There they are. Listen.... Listen.... They're running him in the dark!"

Far away on the hillside a light twinkled suddenly, turning the twilight land into darkness as the first star makes it night in the sky.

Barnaby laughed. "That was a hunt!" he said. "Hark! he's stopped them. We'll have to find our way out of this. Why, we can't see each other's faces.... Let's keep on a bit up this hedge-side, and perhaps we'll get into a bridle-road."

He went first, striking into a kind of track.

"There should be a gate in the corner," he said. "Better let your horse get his head down and smell out the rabbit-holes. We're like the babes in the wood, aren't we? Mind that grip!—Where are you?"

The gate was there. They passed through it, and on the other side was a sign-post. Barnaby struck a match, standing up in his stirrups to peer at the moss-stained board.

"I'm afraid," he said, "we'll be late for that concert. Unless we can strike Kilgour's habitation and get him to send us on. Shall we try for it? We're—oh, never mind where we are; it's the end of the world, anyhow. Are you tired to death?"

He turned round with the match in his fingers, and looked at her, but it had burnt down; he dropped it, and reaching out, caught her hand, swinging it in his as their horses stumbled on side by side.

"What a cold little hand!" he said, but his grip was warming it through the leather....

The end of the world.... He had used the word so lightly, but it called her back to reason. Another day was over. And perhaps to-morrow the world might end.

CHAPTER IX

The Duchess and her friend Wickes were a trifle anxious, but their faces cleared as the late ones arrived. Two or three rows behind them the village schoolmaster dropped like a shot rabbit into his seat.

"A minute later and we'd have been lost," whispered the Duchess. "It's always a battle to keep him off the platform. Once he is wound up no power on earth can stop him. Twice already he has offered his recitation, proposing to fill the breach."

"Poor devil, what a shame!" said Barnaby. "Why not let him?"

"We did let him—once," said Wickes, and a reminiscent shudder passed down the row. He addressed himself eagerly to Susan.

"It's awfully good of you, Mrs. Hill," he said, the worried creases in his long face relaxing. "Every time I get up a village concert I swear it will be the last, but I go on doing it year by year. You have no idea what the tribulations are——"

"That is meant for me," said the Duchess, lowering her voice to a guilty whisper. "—I ask you, how could I help it? You know what a commotion there was this morning, getting off to the meet.—I told somebody to call down from my window to Rufus Brown that he was to attend this concert and sing *John Peel*.—I could tell him a mile off by his old grey horse; you know how the creature bobs his head up and down:——"

"*I* did your bidding," said Barnaby. "You only said 'Stop him!' and I don't know who on earth it was, but it certainly wasn't Rufus."

"How was I to know," groaned the Duchess, "that he had sold the grey?"

"But the beggar was quite delighted," protested Barnaby, who saw nothing worse than a joke in this substitution of a probably voiceless stranger. "He undertook to do it."

The Duchess pointed a solemn finger.

"Barnaby," she said, "you have been out of the world too long. You don't know the whole horror of the position. There he sits!"

"Flushed with victory," murmured someone else, "hoarse with bawling:——"

"It was an awful moment," said the Duchess, "when he came and thanked me for the compliment I had paid him. I've never spoken to the wretch in my life."

"He feels you have adopted him now," said the Job's comforter at her elbow. "Barnaby, you don't know him. He's the most impossible bounder who was ever kicked out of society, and we have all been turning him the cold shoulder for the last two seasons. We were beginning to hope we had finally choked him off."

"Poor Wickes is nearly beside himself," said the Duchess. "He will never get over it. But imagine my feelings when I discovered what I had done— —"

"The populace at the back didn't know what to make of it; they are used to us rollicking in *John Peel*,—shouting out the chorus. But we were all too utterly petrified to emit a whoop— —"

"Is there anything you would like in the way of properties, Mrs. Hill?" said Wickes, in a severe, sad voice. Susan looked down, suddenly nervous, her hands clenched, her face a little pale.

"What is your wife going to do?" Kilgour was asking, and Barnaby was answering carelessly that he didn't know.

"She is rather a dab at acting," he said, and now he was looking humorously at her. But for once she failed to smile back her recognition of the eternal joke between them.... Yes, she was good at acting....

"Turn the lights down," she said, and Mr. Wickes flew obediently to the nearest lamp. Anything to obliterate past misfortunes!—"And there is a woman at the back with a baby. Ask her to lend it to me."

She had meant to amuse them differently, but some impulse had made her change her mind. She flung a dark shawl, borrowed, over her satin frock. Mr. Wickes came back to her, carrying the child gingerly; its mother had relinquished it with pride, only protesting against his taking it up by the back of its neck like a puppy, which Wickes, distracted by his responsibilities, had seemed inclined to do.

They were all looking at her with interest, mildly stirred to expect something unusual, as the anxious Wickes helped her on to the platform and lowered another lamp. But as she stood above them their curious faces faded, and the touch of the little body, so light in her arm, took her out of herself. She was once more playing, playing for life, in the Tragedy Company; making the people sob at the tragic end of the drama.

"—Don't waken the child...."

The first note of her voice vibrated like the plaintive string of a harp. The listeners were startled.

She was the woman whose husband was faithless and, in the horrible madness that gripped him, was coming to take her life. She was shut in, hidden in a poor shelter, miles away from human help; and she was listening for his step in terror, loving him so bitterly still that she would have been glad to die, but clinging desperately to life for the sake of his child. And she rocked the baby on her arm, half distracted; singing to it, ceasing her chant to listen ... and imagining his approach. But all the while, in her despair, she stifled the scream that was on her lips;—she must not waken the child.

Farther and farther she retreated, staring with frightened eyes at the door, but still hushing the baby at her breast; and then, all at once, she stopped, and bent her face to its cheek. A pause hung, significant; and then came her cry, dreadful, heart-breaking. The baby was still. He might come; he might kill her ... he could not waken the child....

"Good heavens, how real!" said Mr. Wickes.

Susan, breathing a little quicker, looked down on the dim-lit audience. All these women could ride, all these women could dance.... She wanted Barnaby to think of her sometimes, later. Would he remember her by the one thing they could not do? by that wild scrap of melodrama?

The room was shaking with an almost hysterical applause. Behind there was an enthusiastic stamping. And the only woman who was not crying was the baby's mother, who was too flattered, and one other who looked on with disdainful eyes.

"Did you like it?" asked the actress wistfully. It was Barnaby himself who had come forward to help her down. She could not hear what he said; it was under his breath, and it was drowned in the clapping.

The lights had gone up again; she could recognize the people who were surrounding her, as she stepped down amongst them. Near the wall, not very far from the Duchess, who was frankly borrowing a large, masculine handkerchief, were sitting a thin, fair woman, and a big, stupid, slow-witted man. They both had an odd look of having just found each other. The Duchess wagged her head at them.

"Yes," she whispered, "there they are. They have made it up.... Wickes, don't you think it would be a noble deed to invite the schoolmaster to play God Save the King? It will get his name into the local paper."

"Certainly," said Wickes. He took a long breath, conceiving his troubles over, remaining, however, with his eyes fixed on Susan in a kind of awed curiosity. Finally he spoke out the problem in his mind.

"Do you mind telling me," he said, apologetically, "what spell you used—how you contrived to keep the infant quiet?"

"Oh, she's a witch!" said Barnaby.

"Yes, she's a witch," said the Duchess kindly, "but I know the secret. It had a comforter in its mouth."

They were all moving now, bustling out of their chairs, and blocking up the gangway with their "good nights." The proletariat was waiting for them to depart before shuffling out of the shilling benches. And there was Julia, paler than usual, but as lovely, smiling at Barnaby, giving him a long, strange look that was full of pity and understanding....

"You're done up," said Barnaby. "Come along. I shouldn't have let you be dragged into this performance on the top of a hard day's hunting."

She kept her lip steady, wishing she had not seen that interchange of glances; shrinking absurdly from the implication that was conveyed by Kilgour's officious interposition of his broad person. Did he think he could arrest the march of events by planting himself like a kind ox between Barnaby and Julia? Did he think they

CHAPTER IX 87

would not find means—? Still she kept her lip steady, letting Barnaby hurry her down the room; reminding herself that she had no right to feel insulted, or even a little sad.

*****

When they reached home she was going straight upstairs, as was her custom, but Barnaby stopped her.

"Don't go up yet," he said. "You ate no dinner. I told them we'd have something when we came in."

She let him draw a chair for her beside that red fire in the hall that always tempted the weary to go no farther; and bring things that she did not want out of the dining-room.

"I've sent away the servants," he said. "I've got out of the way of them flitting round me. You'd rather sit here, wouldn't you, and get warm and let me forage?"

For a little while they were gay, and then he cleared away plates and glasses, and a silence fell between them. He settled down in another of the great chairs and lit a cigarette. A smile curved in the corners of his mouth and vanished; he was thinking hard. Susan watched him, shading her eyes with her hand that he might not raise his head suddenly and read their wistfulness. She was not often alone with him in the house.

What was he thinking? His face was no longer careless; the kind blue eyes were fixed earnestly on the fire. She remembered the strangeness of Julia's look and her heart ached, guessing. Something must have happened between them; he must have let her see unmistakably that he loved her still. For there had been no restlessness in Julia's air, no bravado,—it had been the smile of a woman who was sure. And he had himself set a barrier between them.

She felt a wild longing to comfort him, to take his head on her arm and whisper that nothing was too hard for a man,—nothing worth that steadfast, unhappy gaze.

He moved, and the start it gave her set her pulses beating fast. If he had not stirred, might not the impulse have been too much for her? might she not have found herself kneeling by him, comforting him in the madness of her heart? She heard her own voice, imploring, sharp as if in some stress of mortal fright—

"Oh, let me go! Oh, will you not let me go?"

He had looked up quickly. The sobbing wildness of her cry broke in on his absent mood.

"You are tired of the farce?" he said.

She came back to herself. What was the matter with her? "I—cannot—bear it," she said slowly.

And for a minute there was silence again between them. She heard the fire crackling, a far-away clock ticking on the stairs; ... she thought she could hear the silence itself.

"I didn't know it was hurting you," he said.

He was sorry for her; he must not be sorry. She tried to laugh.

"Don't think of me," she said. "It—it didn't matter. After all, I'm an actress. I am one of these strange people that can pretend. Let me go back to the other kind of acting, where nobody will think me real; where there will be crowds applauding, and not just one person to be amused and say—'She carries it off well, but she'll make a slip,—she will stumble!' ... Oh, it couldn't hurt me. Don't you know we can only hurt ourselves?"

"Do you think I'll let you go back to that life?" he said.

His voice recalled the raging warmth of pity with which he had once referred to his lawyer's tale of her plight. Apparently the situation still roused in him a mistaken feeling that she was in his charge. She flushed, struggling with a betraying weakness.

"A hard life," she said, "but not unbearable.... My public will not be cheated. They will not shame me with too much kindness——"

Barnaby was not listening.

"Who was the man,—that fellow last night?" he said.

Why did he speak of that? Did he dare to imagine that she was building on another man's promises? that she was scheming, calculating—?

"No,—" she cried bitterly. "No,—not that!"

A great while after, it seemed to her, he spoke again. His voice was quiet.

"I think you are right," he said. "It's time to make an end of this. It's too dangerous."

"Yes," she said faintly. That at least was true....

He went on, rather quickly. She was not looking at him. She could not.

"Listen. To-morrow you'll have a wire from London. I'll see to it. I'm afraid we can't make it a cable; there isn't time. It will have to be from my lawyers, saying you are wanted in America on important business. My mother doesn't understand business. Anyhow, you'll be excited, and you needn't know what it means; so you can't explain."

"Yes," she said, in the same low voice. "To-morrow."

"We'll have to see about boats and things when we get up to town. And, of course, we'll have to make up a story. But once you're out of this country——"

Yes, once she was out of this country it would all be simple. She had only to disappear.

"What will you say of me?" she asked, with a sad quaintness. "Will you tell them that I am dead?"

He moved suddenly, checking himself.

"Oh, God knows!" he said. "It will take a lot of planning. You've forgotten the—other lady."

Yes, that was his difficulty. Although she would be gone there would still be a bar between him and Julia. That was the tragedy.

"I'll be out when the wire comes, probably," he said. It seemed to amuse him to settle the details; he seemed to be flinging his seriousness aside. "Rackham is coming over to try a horse. For form's sake you'll have to send for me immediately. I'll be somewhere down in the schooling pastures."

The nearness of exile took away her breath. But the impossible situation could only have ended so. That had been their bargain. At least she had not failed him, she had done all that he asked of her, drinking the bitter cup of her own dishonesty to the dregs. A rush of memory carried her back to that first night of his return, so distant, and yet such a little while ago. She held out her hand to him, humbly, uncertainly—

"Good night," she said. "You—you have been good to me."

Barnaby took her hands in his; clasped them hard. It was surely not his voice that was so unsteady.

"It's the last time, is it?" he said. "Let's play it out gallantly. Let's pretend. Susan,—Susan—is that how you say good night to your husband?"

Her heart beat fast; her head was dizzy. He was looking down in her eyes, drawing her hands to his breast.

No, not Barnaby:—not the one man she trusted!...

"Good night,—Sir," she whispered.

And he remembered; he let her go and stood back as she passed him on her way to the stairs.

"Good night," he repeated, in that queer, unsteady voice. "I beg your pardon,—Madam."

CHAPTER X

To-morrow had come.

It was the same kind of morning as other mornings; there was no lurid conflagration lighting up the sky. Outside it was dull and quiet, and even the wind was still. Susan paused at the staircase window, gazing a little while.

In the hall beneath she heard Barnaby talking to the dogs. And his voice shook her. The stunned sense of finality that was with her gave way to a sharp and sudden pain.

She could not bear to go down to him. Turning, she fled back.

"Is that you, Susan?" called Lady Henrietta. She was sitting up at her breakfast, and the door of her room was ajar. "Where is Barnaby riding out so early? I heard his boots creaking as he went by."

"I don't know," the girl said, truly. "I haven't seen him."

"Then don't loiter like a draught in the door," said Lady Henrietta impatiently. "Come in and have your tea up here and help me to read my letters."

She did as she was bidden. The sharp kindliness of Barnaby's mother was sweet to her; and it was the last time she would sit with her, the last time she would listen with a smile that was not far from tears to her caustic prattle. Whatever happened to her, however they managed her disappearance, she and Lady Henrietta would never meet again. Would she think of her sometimes,—kindly?—She was not to know....

"What's the matter now?" said Lady Henrietta suddenly. "You look pale."

Hurriedly the girl defended herself from the imputation.

"Of course, it's Barnaby," said Lady Henrietta, undismayed. "I suppose he has been behaving badly."

"Oh no! Oh no!" cried Susan.

Lady Henrietta waved her hands impatiently. How fragile she looked, how pretty;—the pink in her cheekbones matching her painted silk peignoir. The hardness that sometimes marred her expression had softened to a pitying amusement, and she had a look of Barnaby when she smiled like that.

"You'd deny it with your last gasp," she said.

Susan was picking up and arranging the letters that were lying in disorder. It was difficult to sustain that quizzical regard. But Barnaby's mother had not finished with her. She was not to be distracted.

"You never tell me anything, either of you," she said. "What is a mother-in-law for but to rule the tempest and shoot about in the battle? It's too firmly fixed in your heads that I am a brittle thing, and whatever is raging round me I am not to be excited. And it's absurd. I don't mind having a heart,—in reason. It's amusing; a kind of trick up my sleeve. But I won't have it robbing me of my rightful flustrations.—I am as strong as a horse, if you two would realize it. And you and Barnaby are such a funny couple."

She scanned the girl's face a minute.

"I'm attached to you, you little wretch," she said. "But I don't believe you care a straw for him."

But as she spoke her merciless eyes had pierced the girl's mask of light-heartedness. On this last morning Susan was not mistress of herself.

"You *are* fond of him!" she said. "Dreadfully, ridiculously fond of him like any old-fashioned girl...."

"Oh, hush!" cried Susan. Anything to stop that unmerciful proclamation. She flung herself on her knees, and her terrified protest was stifled in Lady Henrietta's arms.

"How silly we are!" said she, but she held the girl tightly. "I'm to bridle my tongue, am I? You are afraid I shall tell him? Oh, you poor little girl, you baby, is it as bad as that?"

She pushed her away, as if ashamed of her own emotion, and a fierceness came into her voice, that had been entirely kind.

"If you allow that woman to ruin your lives—!" she said. "Oh, I'm not blind, I'm not altogether stupid—! If you let her take him from us—I'll never forgive you, Susan."

Having launched her bolt, all unconscious of its stabbing irony, she recovered her bantering equanimity, and looked whimsically at her listener.

"Why are you gazing at me," she said, "as if I were about to vanish? I'm not going to die of it. I am going to take the field."

*****

Barnaby was not in the house when the girl went at last downstairs. She wandered in and out of the library, trying to smother her expectation, listening without ceasing for the telegram that was to come and make an end. He did not appear at luncheon, and she sat alone, pretending to eat, but starting at every sound. Afterwards, to quiet her restlessness, she went round to the stables to say good-bye to the horses.

The pigeons flew down to her as she walked into the wide flagged yard. She went to the corn bin and scattered a handful as they circled round her and settled at her feet. The men must be still at dinner. There was no stud groom to look reproachful as she tipped a little oats in a sieve to give secretly to the horse that had been her own in this country of make-believe. She felt like a thief as she lifted the latch. It seemed wrong to be there by herself, without Barnaby. She had always gone round with him.

The horse lifted his beautiful head, and they stared at each other. She patted his quarter with her flat hand, and he went over and let her empty her parting gift in his manger.

"Good-bye," she said. "Good-bye, old boy!"

Tears choked her. She stumbled out through the straw and shut the door on him.

All down that side of the yard there was a row of boxes. The bay came first, and then the chestnut that Barnaby had ridden yesterday afternoon. He pulled a little with Barnaby; ... he had never pulled with her. And there was the hotter chestnut that she had called Mustard, and the brown horse that had been mishandled and had a trick of striking out when a stranger came up to him in the stall. She had gone with Barnaby to look at him when he first arrived from the dealers',—and Barnaby had caught her back just in time. The horse looked at her gravely, sadly, with no evil flicker in his eye. Life had dealt hardly with him as with her, and he seemed, best of them all, to understand. But Barnaby had forbidden her to go near him.... Mechanically she went on to Black Rose's box, but her place was empty.

There was a grey next door, an old horse that had carried her many times. He was to be fired in the spring, sold perhaps. She leant her head, shuddering, against him; and he licked at her hand like a dog.... What was the end of them, all these brave, patient, willing creatures? A few seasons' eager service, and then, step by step, as the tired muscles failed the undying spirit—knocking from hand to hand, harder fare, worse misusage,—the dreadful descent into hell.

Once, on their way back from hunting, they had come suddenly on a strange procession, a gaunt herd of worn-out shadows making their last journey, staggering humbly along the wayside. It was a haunting tragedy. Staring ribs, hollow eyes dim with misery,—and the cursing driver thrashing one that had fallen, and lay in a quivering heap on the grass. She had asked what this horror was.... Just a shipload of useless horses travelling in the dusk their unspeakable pilgrimage to the sea.

And she had turned on the men riding at her side. Shame on them, that were English, that called themselves a sporting nation.... What a lie that was! she had cried....

And Barnaby had said—"She's right there!" and the other men had not laughed....

There were voices in the saddle-room. One of the grooms crossed the yard whistling. She was still leaning her head against the old horse, and she waited. She did not want the men to stare at her and wonder; she did not want them to find her there.

"The master took out Black Rose, didn't he?"

CHAPTER X

"Yes. He's gone down the fields with his Lordship."

"Will he be riding her in the Hunt steeplechases?"

That was a stranger's voice, not one of Barnaby's servants.

"Can't say."—The stud groom was cautious.

"That's an ugly brute of his Lordship's. Why didn't he ride him here?" said another voice, joining in.

"He had to go somewhere in the motor, and so I'd orders to bring the horse over. It wasn't a job I envied," said Rackham's groom.

"If ever a horse was a devil, that one is," said the stud groom, laconically.

"Wants a devil to back him," muttered Rackham's man. "I never ride out of our yard without expecting he'll down me. Got a history, hasn't he?"

"Who told you that?"

"Stevens told me you'd passed a remark about him."

The stud groom received the insinuating suggestion with a dignity that was proof against pumping for the space of a minute. He chewed on a straw discreetly. Then his own knowledge became too much for him.

"If I told you his history, Arthur Jones," he said slowly, "you'd never lay your legs across him no more."

"Then for God's sake tell it," said Arthur Jones.

The stud groom laughed grimly. He was a man of saturnine humour, and liked impressing his underlings.

"His Lordship knows," he said. "If any man could cow a horse, he can. Weight tells. Weight and devilry. But any other gentleman buying Prince John I'd call it suicide. If I didn't,—according to circumstances, mind you"—he lowered his voice, not much, but enough—"call it murder."

Would the men never stop gossiping and disperse? She would have to face their curious looks at last.

"I was up Yorkshire way when his Lordship bought him," said the stud groom deliberately. "Four of us was leaning over the bars at that auction. Two of us had a mourning band on the sleeve of our coats, and the third chap had unpicked the crape off his a month ago. When they put Prince John in the ring there came a frost on the bidding. They said he'd ought to 'a been shot out of the road, and never put up for sale. His name wasn't Prince John then. He'd been run in two 'chases, owners up;—and he'd killed them both."

The men stood with their mouths open, digesting the horrid tale. And a stable lad ran into the yard from his vantage point on a hillock.

"They're down at the jumps," he said, "—and they're changing horses."

It was then that the girl came out, passing swift as an apparition. The men fell back, touching their caps.

"I'll lay she heard you," said Rackham's man.

The stud groom looked after her curiously and, crossing over to the door of the grey's box, that she had left unfastened, closed it without a word.

She did not know why she was hurrying to the house. What half-conscious panic had seized her as her inattentive mind took its wandering impression of the grooms' idle gossip? What words had reached her, lodging in her brain to inspire that wild sense of impending trouble? It was no good searching for Barnaby in the house. He was down at the jumps,—changing horses.

"There's a wire for you," said Lady Henrietta.

It had come. At first she looked at it stupidly, as if it, the signal, were some trivial interruption. She heard herself explaining, like an unthinking scholar repeating a half-forgotten lesson. "I must go away. I—I have to go away."

"Bad news?" asked Lady Henrietta quickly. Susan crumpled the telegram in her hand.

"Yes, it's bad news," she said. "It is from the lawyers."

Vaguely she recollected what she was to say. Something about going up to London at once, and perhaps on to America.

"Let me see it," said Lady Henrietta. "Yes, it sounds urgent. We'd better send somebody to fetch Barnaby. He will have to take you. You must catch the afternoon train."

"Yes, I must catch the afternoon train," repeated Susan. That was decided. Had not Barnaby mapped it out? She wondered dully how he had managed to convey private instructions for that impeccable message; but all the while she was thinking, thinking,—and suddenly she was conquered by her wild, unreasoning fear for him.

"I'll go and find him," she said.

Lady Henrietta demurred, curious, desiring to cross-examine; but the girl's face smote her, and she forbore to hold her back.

It was not far down the fields, and she went like a driven leaf, possessed by a fear that would not be stilled by reason. She had gone down there sometimes to watch them schooling hunters, and she had ridden the jumps herself, that day when Barnaby showed her how they trained steeplechasers, with real wide hedges and a movable leaping bar. He had tried to prevent her risking the double, bristling with difficulty, and she had defied him, larking over it, and then galloping back to him to say she was sorry.

She counted the fences mechanically as they came up one by one, visible against the winter sky; lines of artificial ramparts, defended by a guard rail, made up with furze;—and the lapping rim of that actual water jump. The strange thing was that as she came nearer and nearer, instead of diminishing, her premonition grew. She talked to herself to keep down her panic.

Why were so few men killed steeplechasing? Because it was dangerous, Barnaby had said. It was the rabbit holes and the mole-hills and the grips that broke your neck unawares.... That was the gate he had shut between them, he sitting on his horse on the far side laughing, while she practised hooking the latch and pushing it back with the handle of her whip. He had shown her first the nail studded in the horn of the handle to keep it from slipping;—and then he had clapped the gate shut, declaring that till she opened it fairly, without his help, she should never pass. And she had ridden through triumphantly at last. It was the only thing he had had to teach her. How quaint they were, these heavy wooden latches.... She let the gate swing and ran.

Rackham was on Black Rose, and Barnaby on a chestnut. They were walking their horses when she caught sight of them, and Barnaby was letting his look over a fence, flicking his whip at the ridge of furze with its withering yellow blossom. They were not talking loud, but she thought his voice sounded angry. The chestnut was restive.

"Keep still, you brute!" he said.

Something was wrong between the two men. Some old antagonism had flared up, rousing them to a hot discussion. The chestnut lifted his forefeet off the ground, and Barnaby shook his bridle carelessly, warning him again to be quiet. Then all at once up he went, seizing the unguarded moment....

Crash!

The girl saw him rise, saw him stagger, falling back on his rider; and she ran on with sobbing breath.

The chestnut rolled over sideways and struggled on to his legs. A little way off the mare was plunging, upset by what was happening; she could hardly be controlled. Susan had reached Barnaby, she had thrown herself down beside him to lift his head from the rough grass where he lay so still. Rackham had dismounted; he was coming to help;—but she was out of her mind with terror. She caught up Barnaby's whip, springing to her feet, lashing at him as if he were a wild beast that she must keep at bay. Then she dropped on her knees again, and laid her cheek on Barnaby's heart, and the turf was heaving up round them both.

Far off, indistinct, she heard troubled whispers, and one quite close.

"He's breathing still, my lady." (That was the stud groom, who had formerly served a countess. He always addressed her so.) She looked up at him.

"He's living yet, my lady," the man repeated in an awed undertone. "Best not try to move him. They've sent a car for the doctor. Best let him lie till they come...."

He knelt on the other side, and one of the men stood over him in his shirtsleeves, folding up his coat. With significant carefulness they raised Barnaby's head a little and slipped it under. And then they all waited and watched for a hundred years....

When the doctor came he was still unconscious. Something was broken, and there was bad concussion. It was possible he might be injured internally, strained, crushed,—a cursory examination could not make sure. They stripped a hurdle of its furze, and he was lifted and laid upon it; the men hoisted it on their shoulders and tramped with a dreadful slowness through the fields to the house.

"I'll ride on and break it to his mother," said Rackham, averting his eyes from Susan as he spoke to her.

"Yes," she said dully. She had forgotten him.

And as it often is, the one who was thought least fitted to support a shock took it coolly. A lengthy experience of hunting accidents helped her to seize, comforted, on Rackham's report of concussion, and to believe in his blunt assurance that the whole thing was nothing worse than an ordinary spill. A more diplomatic messenger might have terrified her with his gentleness, but she suspected no concealment in a man who, without beating about the bush, looked her right in the face and lied. She did not see the men carry their burden in, and when the others came to her, relieving Rackham, she was comparatively calm. Her active fancy was diverted by measures that she ascribed to a misplaced anxiety for herself.

"I am not going to collapse," she insisted. "It's too ridiculous making this fuss about me and not letting me go to him. It's not the first time the poor boy has been brought back to me knocked silly. You needn't be so fidgety over me;—you had better look after Susan.... My dear, my dear, I know what it is! And concussion is a thing the doctors can't cut you to pieces for, thank Heaven. Give her a little brandy!"

Rackham's glance met the doctor's. The case was too serious to provoke a smile.

Lady Henrietta had turned to Susan.

"Oh," she said, with the air of one who wished to demonstrate to an over-anxious circle that she had her wits about her—"that telegram—! Of course you can't go now. We must wire up to town.—"

The girl listened to her without at first comprehending.

"Oh,—the telegram," she repeated. How pathetically absurd that futile invention sounded now.

"I must go to him," she said.

The doctor nodded encouragement.

"I'll bring a nurse back with me when I come again," he promised.

Into the girl's pale cheek came a sudden colour. She lifted her head and her eyes shone. She held out her hand, and all at once it was steady.

"No one else;—no one but me!" she cried.

Oh, the farce was not played out; the curtain was not down. She was still his wife to that audience; it was to her he belonged, to no other.... Desperately she stood on her rights;—the poor, fictitious rights she had purchased with all that pain.

"*You* can't nurse him," the doctor was saying gently. "You'd break down; you would make yourself ill. You don't know what you would be undertaking."

But Barnaby's mother was on her side.

"Fiddlesticks!" said she. She had brightened unaccountably; in her voice ran a queer little tremor of satisfaction. "Let her make herself ill if she likes. Why shouldn't she? I've no patience with modern vices, calling in hirelings—! A wife's place is with her husband, not quaking outside his door."

Susan was looking bravely in the doctor's doubtful face.

"You can trust me," she said, on her pale lips a wistful flicker that hardly was a smile.—"I too was a—hireling, once. I know how."

She knew he must yield. What man would dare to stop her? What man would dare to dispute her claim? Only Barnaby himself, who might one day laugh at the tragic humour of her assumption. A kind of despairing joy shook her soul, and was blotted in a passionate eagerness of devotion. Barnaby was hurt, perhaps dying, ... and nothing could conjure her from his side.

CHAPTER XI

The house had become very quiet.

Under Barnaby's windows and right down the avenue the crunching granite was spread with tan. The servants moved silently about their work, even in the far kitchens whence not a sound could be heard.

For a long time he was unconscious; for a long time he lay breathing heavily, and they could not tell if he was in pain. Other doctors came down from London, and Lady Henrietta had to be told what it was that the girl was fighting with that pale and steady face.

"It's love, sheer love, that keeps her going," said one witness to another, watching her courage in the deeps of agony and uncertainty, and, at last, in the breakers of hope.

She was safe in giving herself without stint, because for a long while he did not know her, and it did not matter to him who it was that was soothing him with a passionate gentleness of which his jarred brain would have no knowledge when it recovered its normal tone. She could sit at his bedside hushing him, whispering that she loved him, she loved him, and he must sleep.

Sometimes he talked to her in unintelligible mutterings, sometimes his rambling speeches, without beginning or end, were bitter to understand.

"You mustn't mind what he says," the doctor warned her kindly. "It's certain to be rubbish. Generally they go over and over some silly thing they remember.—I had a patient once who got into fearful trouble through winding off something about a murder he had read in a book."

—That was after he had stood awhile listening gravely to Barnaby's restless talk.

—"I'll find a way out. Wait a bit, my darling.... We'll not have our lives ruined by that mad marriage. I'll find a way out for us."

It was not always the same. Sometimes in the night it would be—"I tell you she's my wife. No, no, not the other. Awfully good joke, what? Mustn't lose my head, though; mustn't lose my head."

And Susan would lay her cheek against his in an agony lest he should hurt himself with his excitement.

"Sleep!" she would whisper, "oh, my dearest, lie still and sleep...."

"But I love her. Don't you know that? I can't marry my girl. Because I love her;—just because I love her—mustn't lose my head!"

Once after she had quieted him, and he had lain a little while motionless he called her.

"Are you there?" he said. His voice was so sensible that she trembled.

"Yes," she said softly, and he gave a sigh of content. But soon he was muttering again, and restless.

"She wants me to sleep," he was repeating, "she wants me to sleep."

No, he had not known who she was. She bent over him, smoothing his forehead with a tender and anxious hand. Sometimes her touch was magnetic.

"Yes," she said. "Hush, my dearest."

"Kiss me," he murmured suddenly, "and I'll go to sleep."

And since at all costs he must be coaxed to slumber, she kissed him for the woman who was not there.

*****

Slowly he turned the corner, slowly.

And at last she found him watching her one morning as she came towards him with a cup in her hand, across the great, wide room. She liked this room; it was so vast and simple. Its battered furniture must have been his when he was a boy. And there was no clutter of pictures and photographs; only a few ancient oil-paintings of hounds and horses. Above his bed a square patch in the wall-paper that was unfaded, betrayed where a woman's portrait had hung once and had been taken down.

"Hullo!" he said.

He lay looking at her, thin and haggard, but his whimsical smile unchanged.

"It's she," he said, "or is it the stuff that dreams are made of?"

"It is she," said Susan.

"I've been ill, haven't I?" he said. "And I say, Susan, have you been nursing me?"

"Yes," she said, steadily.

"I thought so. I've had a kind of feeling that you were there. What's it all about? Wasn't I down at the jumps with Rackham,—and the horse went up—? Did I get damaged?"

"Rather," she said.

"And you didn't fly to America?"

"No," she said.

His weak, amused voice, talking in pauses, smote on her heart.

"Ah," said Barnaby. "It would have looked bad if you'd bolted, wouldn't it? No end heartless. Susan,—oh, I've noticed things, off and on,—you've been killing yourself looking after me.—"

His smile was troubled. She shook her head at him.

"You didn't do it," he said, "because, oh,—because of some queer notion that you owed us something—? You didn't do it to make it up to us,—to pay us out?"

She put her arm under his pillow and, raising him slightly, lifted the cup to him and let him drink. If Barnaby could have known:—if he could have seen her claiming him in her hour of desperation—! If he could have dimly guessed what a dreadful happiness had walked hand in hand with pain! She had won something of her mad adventure. She was the woman who had nursed him, who had waked night after night at his pillow. Nobody could rob her of that. And when she was gone he would perhaps think of her with kindness....

"It wasn't remorse," she said.

"It's awfully good of you," said Barnaby. "But why—but why——" There was a faint eagerness in his puzzled voice.

"Perhaps," she said bravely, "it was the dramatic instinct. How could a poor actress forget all her traditions? How could she help rising to her part? Don't talk.... Lie quiet and laugh at me all you want."

*****

One day Lady Henrietta came into the room with a budget of letters and all she could rake of gossip.

"You two have been shut up so long," she said, "I believe you have both forgotten there is such a thing as an outside world. Why don't you ask who has been inquiring for you?"

"Who has been inquiring for me?" said Barnaby.

He was propped high in his pillows, and was looking like himself. In the afternoon he was to dress and sit in a chair and read the paper.

"Everybody," she said. "Poor Rackham has been two or three times a day when you were bad. Of course it was his horse that did the mischief. He would not be satisfied without seeing Susan——"

"Did you see him?" asked Barnaby. There was something a little odd in his intonation.

"Susan see anybody?" exclaimed his mother. "She had eyes for nobody but her patient. All the wild horses in Rackham's stables would not drag her away from you.—He's thinking of going abroad for a bit, he says. To America, or Canada;—he confused me with his talk of cities and mines and mountains. I don't know if he has any idea of making a fortune there or if he is looking out for a lady. I said you might have to go out there too, but the unfortunate accident had postponed it,—and he said it was a bigger place than I fancied, but to let him know if he could be of any use to you. His manner was rather queer."

"Poor chap," said Barnaby. "I daresay he is hard up. It would have been lucky for him if I—Why, what is the matter, Susan?"

"Don't tease her," said Lady Henrietta. "You can't possibly realize what a fright she had!" She turned briskly to the girl, however. "We never heard any more of that mysterious telegram that was to carry you off so quickly the day Barnaby was hurt," she said. "Have you quite forgotten it? Does absolutely nothing matter to you but him?"

Barnaby had begun to laugh, weakly, uncontrollably.

"Oh, that will keep," he said.

"What do you know about it?" said Lady Henrietta, catching him up sharply. "It came when you were out. I understood she was looking for you when she witnessed your smash. And I'm convinced it has never entered her head from that day to this."

Then she remembered her heap of letters.

"Look at all these!" she cried. "All begging for news of him! And the offerings! There never was anything so romantic.... There's one old woman down in the village that's killed her pig and, Barnaby—she sent up a delicate bit in a dish for you."

"Romantic—?" said Barnaby.

"Oh, romance has singular manifestations," said Lady Henrietta. "You never know.... There was that girl of Bessy's, for example, who used to write poetry.—She was too romantic, poor thing, and that's why she never married.—She went in for hero-worship. Used to go into kind of trances of adoration over a famous soldier that she had never seen. And once I tumbled over her sitting on the hearthrug with her hands clasped behind her head, gazing with a rapt expression into the fire. I thought she was fighting his battles with him in her imagination, or poetising; but she whispered—'Don't interrupt me! I'm darning his socks.—'"

She was turning over her letters.

"Here's one for you, Susan," she said. "It's a London postmark. A big hotel, but rather a common hand."

Susan took it indifferently. Lady Henrietta was already plunged in the midst of a family letter; wherein an aunt of Barnaby's was presuming to offer her advice. She read out bits of it with little shrieks of scorn.

"'When Toby broke his leg I made a point of——' Who cares what folly she committed when Toby broke his leg? 'I do hope, Henrietta, you see that the doctors do not permit the poor boy's wife to be in and out of the sick-room. It irritates the nurses.' ... Ah, but ours is a romantic sick-room! If *we* had married a fool like Charlotte's daughter-in-law—!"

She glanced up smiling at the other two. Providence, not she, had taken the field; and she had faith in its workings as efficacious. But Susan was not attending. She was reading her letter still. "My dear," said Lady Henrietta, "who is the common person?"

But she got no answer.

"Come! Tell us," said Barnaby; and at his voice Susan started.

"Somebody I—used to know," she said.

Lady Henrietta had returned to her own correspondence. Her mild curiosity could wait until the girl had finished deciphering the almost illegible scrawl.

"You might straighten the pillows for me," said Barnaby.

She tore the letter across and threw it into the fire. Then she came over to him and did what he wanted with a jealous eagerness that was new.

"Was it a worrying letter?" he said, in a low voice. He had nothing to do but look at her.

"No," she said, "it didn't worry me." But her tone was subdued, too quiet, as if she had had a shock.

"I'm eternally grateful to you for burning it, though," he said; "that abominable scent it reeked with was like a whiff of nightmare. I seem to remember it. I wonder where I can have run across a woman who advertised herself like that.... I'm glad you burnt it. Considerate nurse. It was the only thing to do."

She was grateful to him for not insisting. Not yet, not yet; not just this morning! ... Afterwards she would tell him.... She moved away from his side and picked up a newspaper from the pile that lay with the letters.

"Do you know what you look like?" said Lady Henrietta, tapping her cheek. "Like a child that has been startled, like a child when an unkind shake has scattered its house of cards."

It was true. But such a tottering house, such a dream-built, precarious house of cards!—

Lady Henrietta dropped her voice, ostensibly to communicate a paragraph in the aunt's letter that was unsuited to the profane masculine understanding.

"I don't want to pry," she said; "but was that by any chance an anonymous letter?"

"Oh, no, no, it was not," said Susan.

"Not Julia's hand disguised? That woman is capable of anything. She's been here several times inquiring. Sending in brazen messages!—"

"Is there anything in the paper?" said Barnaby.

Susan glanced hastily up and down the sheet. No, there was nothing. Among the theatrical announcements an American play that had come to London.

"She is looking in the advertisements!" said Lady Henrietta, affectionately scornful. "My dear, the poor boy is thirsting for murders and politics."

The advertisements.... And among them——

"To-night at 8.

"The Great American Comedy—'Shut Your Windows' ... Mr. Rostiman's Company. Mr. Hayes, Mr. Vine..." (a long list of names that were unknown to her, and un-

CHAPTER XI

meaning);—"*And Miss Adelaide Fish.*"

*****

Barnaby was up and dressed.

He was much amused at his own weakness, at his dependence on that slim, supporting arm. He let Susan settle him carefully in a chair, and then frightened her by getting on to his feet and pretending to walk out of the room. She flew to him, scared, reproachful, making him lean his weight on her shoulder as she brought him back.

"Tyrannical girl!" he said.

She looked down on him as he sat there, dressed and shaved, his clothes fitting rather loosely, his blue eyes hollow. How unspeakably dear he was. How hard to face emptiness....

"I'll put your mother in charge of you while I am gone," she said.

"Don't be too long," said Barnaby. "I'll miss you."

Unwillingly her heart sank. He would miss her. In that little while; in that scant half-hour—!

"Patient," she said, "you flatter."

And smiled at him bravely, and went away.

"I'll go to him immediately," said Lady Henrietta. She was writing furiously, despatching a counterblast to the aunt's interfering letter, which had contained more warnings than she had read aloud. It deserved six pages.

"How do you spell inseparable?" she asked, hardly interrupting the delightful business of administering a slap to one whose daughters-in-law were not wax and whose sons were wild. Distractedly she glanced at Susan.

"You look wan," she said. "I told them you were to have the motor with the hood off. Get all the air you can. Do you mind taking this old brooch into the town to be mended?" Her eyes twinkled as she unpinned it and put it in Susan's hand.

"There!" she said, "that will make sure you don't hurry back too soon, pretending you have had your breath of air."

The girl went into her own room and slipped on a hat and coat. While she tied a veil round her head she remembered that in the diamond star, which was the only thing in the house that was her own, a stone was loose. Since she must go in to the jeweller's on Lady Henrietta's trumped-up errand she might as well take it with her.

The motor was not round when she descended, and she sank into one of the deep chairs in the hall. When she was away from Barnaby the strength in her seemed to fail. It had been heavily tried, and the strain was telling on her, now that it was relaxed.

The tan that had been scattered on the avenue still deadened the sound of wheels. But she saw Macdonald, who was waiting to pack her into the car, moving to the door; and rising, she went towards it. She had not time to draw back as she saw her mistake, for Julia was on the steps.

Swift in seizing her opportunity the visitor walked in at the open door. There was something belligerent in her entrance.

"How is he?" she asked, without preamble, addressing Susan. Macdonald had fallen back discreetly.

"He is better," said Susan coldly. "I have to go out, Miss Kelly."

"I must see him," said Julia, in a low, intense voice that would not be denied. "I've tried and tried, but they never would let me in. You will take me to him."

"*I*?" said Susan.

Julia did not blench under these accents of proud surprise.

"Yes," she said. "You daren't refuse me. I know too much."

The assurance in her voice warned the girl that this was no hysterical vapouring, but a challenge. She answered her bravely, maintaining an outward calm.

"I am sorry I cannot do as you wish," she said.

How lovely the woman was, with her angry flush, and her long-lashed eyes. How recklessly she spoke. Some theatrical impulse in her had overridden prudence; whoever liked might have heard her.... With that odd irrelevance that keeps the mind steady under fire Susan was wondering who it was that had said—"Yes, she's a beauty, but the back of her neck is common——"

"You have no right to keep us apart," said Julia. "I've been patient ... but this is too much! After all I'm not stone; I'm a woman—With all the world gabbling about you and your devotion—! I daresay you think you are getting an influence over him. Poor Barnaby—! All this while you have had him at your mercy!"

She fixed her eyes on Susan with an indescribable stare of scorn.

"Will you take me to him?" she said.

"I will not," said Susan.

Julia came nearer. They were practically alone. Macdonald was putting rugs in the motor.

"I believe you are fond of him," she said ruthlessly. "Fond of him! You the cheat, you the impostor—!"

Ah,—she had known what was coming. She had read it in Julia's eyes. Desperately she stood her ground.

"You insulted me once before," she said slowly.

"Yes," said Julia. "Even then I was not blinded.... But now I know. I've known ever since the Hunt Ball, when Barnaby——"

"Barnaby—?" Susan repeated the word under her breath as if it was strange to her.

"—When Barnaby said that you were not his wife."

CHAPTER XI

The girl stretched out her hands unconsciously for a support that she did not find. There was a mist between them, and she swayed on her feet. Weak in spirit and body from her long nursing, she felt as if someone had struck her a whirling blow. In a kind of vision she saw Barnaby and Julia dancing;—always Barnaby and Julia dancing;—people had talked that night; they had sympathized with her.... Well might Julia laugh at her disapproving world if he had whispered—that! And it was true. She had only to look in Julia's triumphant face to know that this thing was true.

She could not speak. She turned and walked slowly towards the stairs, and began to go up. On the landing above she waited until Julia had reached her side. Then she went along the corridor without turning her head until they had come to the end.

At Barnaby's door she stopped and, turning the handle, spoke at last to the other woman, the woman to whom he had betrayed her.

"Go to him," she said.

And without another word she left her, and left the house.

Barnaby looked up, surprised.

Susan must have started, and Lady Henrietta would not open his door so slowly. Who was this rustling on his threshold?

She took a little run into the room, and stopped.

"Oh, Barnaby!" she cried emotionally. "At last—!"

His unresponsiveness was thrown away on her excited mood. Flushed with victory she misread his expression, less like rapture than consternation.

"This is a bit unexpected," he said. "I'm not in very good form, Julia. I'm afraid I must ask you to excuse me—"

"Was I too sudden?" she said. "Ah, poor Barnaby; how you are altered;—how ill you look! Let me do something for you—"

She rushed at him with enthusiasm, casting a glance around her for illumination, and he could but smile at her hasty gesture, not yet grasping its full significance, not realizing the jealous self-assertion that lay behind her bewildering readiness to push him back in his chair, to shake up his pillows, to administer some potion.

"I don't want anything, thanks," he said. He was still grappling with the problem of her appearance.

"Oh—" she cried, desisting, "to think of you, helpless all this time, and in the hands of that woman—!"

"Are you speaking of my wife?" he said.

Julia laughed softly, reproachfully, and let her eyes rest on his.

"Foolish man!" she said. "You might have trusted me. Think what I've had to endure! Wasn't I punished enough for that ancient misunderstanding? Did you think I was so vindictive that you dared not confide in me? But I would have shared your burdens. For your sake I could even forgive your mother."

What was she driving at? His mouth set in a stiff line that might have warned her if she had not been so sure.

"I meant to wait," she said, "to pretend I was ignorant like the rest; to hug the secret till you struggled out of that wicked tangle and came to me. I understand you so well. I knew for whose sake you were trying to avoid a scandal. Oh, Barnaby, how mad it was—and how like you—!"

"Julia," he said, "what do you mean?"

She missed the dangerous note in his voice, too quiet.

"I'm not angry with you—now," she said caressingly. "But, Barnaby, was it fair to me? People are so uncharitable ... they talked cruelly about us. And if I hadn't known that she was not your wife,—if I hadn't known you were free——"

"That's a mistake," he said grimly. "I am not free."

She stared at him. So great was her gift of illusion, so invincible the vanity that in her was the breath of life, that she had put down his stiffness, his strangeness, to the effort to keep his feelings in control. The glad shock of her visit must have been almost too much for him. But what was that he was saying?

"Oh," she burst out. "Don't tell me she has entrapped you! That's what I was afraid of; that's why I felt I must see you at all risks, in spite of all opposition. I knew she would try to take advantage of your weakness while you were her prisoner, while you lay here at her mercy, no match for her—!"

No, he was not strong yet. His forehead was wet and his mouth was dry. He had a curious longing to find himself back in that cool bed yonder.

"Oh, for God's sake," he cried. "Stop talking nonsense!"

His adjuration checked her passionate speech. She remained gazing.

"I don't know," he said slowly, "how you got hold of your—hallucination. I don't know on what grounds you are making that—accusation. Did I hear you say that Susan was not my wife? Don't repeat it."

Julia drew a quick breath of amazement.

"Barnaby!" she gasped, in an incredulous, startled voice.

"Don't repeat it," he said stubbornly. Yes, the old fire was extinguished, the old spell shattered. And still she gazed at him, unable to comprehend. All at once she began to laugh.

"She did not deny it!" she said. "At first she tried to keep me from you, but when I told her I knew all,—that you had confessed it yourself,—she was beaten. Oh, anybody who saw her face would have known the truth!"

She was frightened then. His eyes were so blue and blazing.

"You told Susan," he repeated, "that I—that *I* had said she was not my wife?"

"Yes," she said, still defiant, but quailing a little before his look.

He stood up. He was regarding her with an expression that held no memories of the past. It was all blotted out; no trampled passion, no hidden tenderness stirred in him to excuse her.

"If you were not a woman—!" he said, in an implacable tone that was unknown to her.—"You had better go."

*****

"What a monster I am!" said Lady Henrietta. "How neglectful!—Was I more than five minutes? You'd have rung if you'd wanted me, wouldn't you? Poor boy, were you very dull?"

"It's nearly time for her to come back," he said.

He was looking tired. Getting up had not done him good. Feeling somewhat guilty his mother sat down to amuse him and make up for her lapse by half an hour's brisk attention.

Somehow his curious depression affected her. She, too, began to listen for the motor.

"I told her not to hurry back," she said apologetically, as time went by. "She's been doing far too much. If she doesn't take care of herself now you're better, she will break down."

"Wasn't that the car?" said Barnaby.

But no light step came hurrying up the stairs.

"I'll ask," said Lady Henrietta, and rang. The servant who came knew nothing, and was sent down to make inquiries. She was puzzled by the report.

"I can't understand this!" she said. "Barnaby—they say the car has come back without her."

His look alarmed her. She jumped up quickly.

"I'll see the man myself," she said; "it must be some ridiculous blunder."

She was a long time downstairs. When she came back she was bewildered and indignant.

"They tell me," she said, "that Julia Kelly has been; that she saw Susan before she went out——"

"She came up here," said Barnaby.

"So the servants tell me," she said. "I can hardly believe it—! And the man says that Susan made him drive her straight to the station. He heard her ask when there was a train to London. There is no message—"

Anger was struggling in her voice with apprehension. She looked suspiciously at her son.

"Barnaby—" she said emphatically, "if this is Julia's doing—I'll never forgive either of you!"

He had got on his feet, and stood uncertainly, as if measuring his strength. The look on his face struck her into silence.

"Don't couple me with Julia," he said, setting his teeth. The sweat was glistening like dew on his forehead. "Poor little girl ... poor little girl.... So she's gone. Why, what's the matter with me? What an incapable fool I am!—How am I to go and find her if I can't—walk—straight across a room—?"

CHAPTER XII

All London was placarded with that American play.

It ran through the streets in big letters on the omnibuses; it walked in tilting lines in the gutter; it stared out from all the hoardings with the wide smile of its principal actress ... Adelaide Fish.

And it was the gaudy poster that startled Susan out of the unhappy listlessness that had fallen on her. Facing her suddenly it arrested her wandering step.

Adelaide Fish.... Had the world stood still after all, and was it this morning that she had had a letter...?

"Hideously inartistic," said one passer-by to another.

"Still she's handsome. I've seen her. One of these big women— —"

Yes, it was inartistic. Reds and blues and greens in vivid splashes, and the name writ large. A marvellous jump from the bankrupt shifts of the Tragedy Company to this smiling elevation. And Barnaby was still ignorant. He had not been warned.

She thought of him now. The passionate shame that had caught her up like a flame sweeping all before it had died out. She felt only a kind of wonder at herself, looking back. It was inevitable. The impossible situation could only have ended so.... But in the background all the while was the woman.

She tried to shake off the lassitude of despair. Why had she burned the letter? She had been going to tell Barnaby, although the writer had forbidden her to share its contents with him. It would have been simpler to let him—but no, she could never have put that letter into his hands. Hard enough to look him in the face and tell him what she could repeat;—that the woman who was his wife, the one in whose likeness she had been masquerading, had written, and was in England. But before she had spoken Julia had intervened and the waters of bitterness had closed over her head.

Barnaby must not be left in the dark. She had a wild and sudden longing to do something for him still; one last service. She could find out from this woman what were her intentions towards him and if it were a threat or a promise that had lurked in that ambiguous letter.

She must ask somebody where she was. For the first time she realized her surroundings, the roar of the traffic, the restless street.

*****

Outside the theatre an interminable train of people, wedged tightly, endured with their faces turned towards the gallery stair; another line, reaching far down the pavement and less good-humoured, guarded the entrance to the pit. The lights falling on their faces threw up a singular likeness in expression, a kind of touch-me-not attitude that defied their physical juxtaposition. Squeezed like herrings, their pained endurance was heightened by the universal lack of a smile. And the lines were haunted by a street musician strumming his lamentable tune.

As Susan went up the dark entry she was pursued by unfriendly glances, the quick suspicion that she was a late comer who must be turned back ignominiously in her base attempt to push in at the head of the line. As she vanished inside the stage door there was an interested murmur; here and there a man unbent and asked his neighbour which of them she was. Then there was a click and the crowd went surging forward. The doors were open.

Miss Fish was in her dressing-room.

Like one in a dream the girl was breathing that familiar atmosphere of the theatre. It seemed to shut off for ever all that was yesterday. She stumbled into a little room violently scented, full of blinding light. And a woman swung round and seized her hands.

"There you are!" she said. "I can't kiss you—my face is sticky. I've sent away my dresser. Wait till I shut that door!"

She made a dash and secured it, then pushed Susan into a chair.

"I'll have to make up while I talk," she said. "Go on; go on. I'm mad with curiosity! I am dying to hear it all."

"I had your letter," said Susan.

Adelaide laughed. Her warm voice had a note of banter.

"I didn't know but you had waxed fat like Jeshurun," she said. "Wasn't it he that kicked?—So I wrote that letter. I had to see you. You burnt it? You didn't tell him?"

"He does not know you are here," said Susan. "He has been ill." Her heart was beating painfully hard; the air in this close little room was suffocating her. It was not air....

"Yes?" said Adelaide. "That's how I know about you. My dear, don't tell me! I picked up a picture paper and saw a piece about him and his accident, and his devoted American wife!—I'd so often wondered what became of you. It's tremendous!"

There was admiration in her gaze as she turned unwillingly from her visitor to the glass, smearing her chin as she talked. "I did hear of him being alive," she said. "I saw that in one of our papers, 'English Gentleman Comes Back from the Grave' and so on. I *was* scared when I thought of you. They said what a joy it was to his wife and his mother, and I thought they had been too hasty. But there was never a word more, though I watched the paper. I decided he must have walked into the offices here and said—'I do not desire you to mention this'—I'd heard it was done sometimes by the upper classes. But—!"

Again her face expressed unqualified admiration. "You must have had a nerve," she said, "you poor kitten!"

The girl sprang up, her mouth proud, her eyes imploring.

"Adelaide," she said, "you were good to me once, you—you tried to help me. Won't you believe me when I tell you I am nothing to him? It was all acting, all acting from beginning to end. Never real, never what you said in your letter. I was only staying in his house playing—that—part till I could disappear without scandal."

"What?" said the woman bluntly. "Has he never said to you—'If I can free myself of the other I'll marry you?'"

"Oh, never; never!"

"Then," said Adelaide, "it's not for your sake his lawyers are getting busy, trying to find what they call flaws, trying to break his marriage? They can try.... You didn't know?"

She turned on the girl with a suddenness that took her unawares; read her face.

"He's not playing you fair!" she cried.

It was remarkable, just then, how she resembled Julia. Half dressed as she was, half made-up, her eyes darkened, and scorn on her carmined lip.

"I'll give you a hold over him," she said. "I'll stand by you. Wasn't it all my doing? Who's that knocking?—You can't come in."

Good-nature was back as she turned from the interruption. She smiled indulgently, as one who was hoarding a gift.

"I wouldn't lift a finger for him," she said. "But I'm silly over you. I'll tell you. And you can go back to him and make your bargain."

The girl shut her lips hard. She must listen;—for Barnaby's sake she must listen. The shamed colour ebbed in her cheek.

"I'm not mad, or bad,—at least not to speak of," said Adelaide, "but I'm careless.... Oh, I'll give you your Englishman, child; you needn't look so stricken! I once had a kind of a romance myself. When I was a young thing like you I married myself to a shabby little poet. But I grew tired of him muttering verses and dreaming things upside down; and we had a divorce, and I ran and left him and went on the stage. And all the while that little man kept on writing; and when he'd used up all his poetry, and all the dead kings and queens, he woke up and wrote a play."

A queer pride, not unmixed with tenderness, came into her voice at that.

"What do you think?" she said. "Nothing would move him but that they should find me out and give me the star part. 'I have had her in my mind all these years,' he said, 'and it is she. No one but she shall play it.'—All these years that I had forgotten him, he was building me a ladder—."

She laughed abruptly, banishing sentiment.

"I've done all the talking," she said, "and I must, while you sit there dumb with your big eyes asking me if it's to be the dagger or the bowl. D'you remember when I was Queen Eleanor, and you were the Rosamond, and the boys nearly shouted the roof down, begging you not to drink? Ah, those times, they were funny. I've shot up since, like a rocket into the sky."

Time was running out. Somewhere in the distance there was a blare of music. She had finished making up, and she must let in her dresser.

"Listen to me," she said. "His people haven't the clues to connect a Phemie Watson they never heard of with Adelaide Fish. You'll have the start of them. Make your terms; make your terms before James and I go to housekeeping again.... I daresay he'd never find it out for himself. About that divorce—it was never fixed. The lawyer wanted to go duck-shooting, and I was gone, and James,—why, they're unbusiness-like, these poets!—he says he had always hugged an inextinguishable spark——"

She paused, looking impatiently at her listener, who was so silent.

"Don't you understand?" she said. "I'm no more Mrs. John Barnabas Hill than you are. If you're wise you'll make him marry you to-morrow."

*****

Susan did not know which way to turn when she was in the street. It seemed much darker; it seemed as if she were lost.

She walked blindly on and on. The people were ghosts that were streaming by; their faces that gleamed and passed did not lighten her terrible loneliness. A straw in that human river, she was afraid.

There was a post-office on the other side of the street. She almost ran to it, unconscious of the swift perils of the crossing.

For she must write to Barnaby, and the thought of communicating with him, poignant as it was, had a strange touch of comfort. The bare office became a harbour.

They gave her a letter card, and she wrote at the counter, with the scratching office pen. That was why it was so ill written. It was ridiculous how such a trifle hurt her. Was it not the first and last time she would ever write to him, and did it matter how badly, since it was to tell him that there was no bar between him and Julia? ...

He would be glad to have it....

She held it fast an instant before letting it fall into the yawning slit. She liked holding it in her hand, because it was a link between her and all that lay behind that curtain of loneliness; because it was going to him. In a little while he would touch it, would wonder, perhaps, at the unknown hand, hat poor scribble—! She dropped it in and it went like her own life into the dark.

For awhile she hurried, fighting her choking terror of the emptiness that was left. Why was it worse now than it used to be? She had been in strange cities, she had been friendless.... And somewhere behind in the glitter that mocked the darkness there was still one person who would help her, if she asked help; who would be kind to her lavishly, without understanding. She did not ask herself why it was impossible to turn in her rudderless flight and appeal to the woman from whom she had tried to guard her heart. There was a gulf between her and Adelaide. Little by little the fear driving her seemed to fail, and all other emotions grew indistinct, crushed by an infinite weight of fatigue. At last she could not think, could not suffer. She only wanted to go to sleep.

*****

It was a frost in Leicestershire. There would be no hunting.

That first irrelevant thought struck Susan as she felt the sharpness of the air breathing in on her face. The narrow window above her head had been propped a little way open with a hair-brush, and the curtain that divided her bed from the next was agitated; she had a neighbour who was astir.

With her eyes shut the girl imagined the grass frozen white, and the branches silver; heard the rapping trot of a string of hunters exercising in the long road beneath the park.

But this was not Leicestershire; it was London, and she was lying in a narrow bed in a small square attic. At the foot stood a washing stand, with a jug and basin, at the head a chest of drawers. There was not room for a chair.

Was it last night she had followed a stranger bearing a candle up flights and flights of uncarpeted wooden stairs? The weariness of that pilgrimage obliterated her stupefied sense of relief when the kind, worn woman had consented to take her in, her absurd inclination to sink down on the chair in the passage and fall asleep. She had thought she would never, never cease climbing stairs.

She remembered now.

Lady Henrietta had asked her once, when she and Barnaby had run up for the day to London, to call on an old governess who was ill. "In a sort of lodging-house," she had said. "One of these places where women live in hutches and eat in the basement." And the dreariness of it had haunted her. Somehow she had found her way there again. The old governess was gone, but the manageress recalled her face. They would not have taken her in without luggage at an hotel.

With that came the recollection that she was penniless. The few chance shillings that she had with her she had spent on her railway ticket. She remembered thinking of that in the train;—she remembered finding Lady Henrietta's battered brooch that she had pinned in her dress to take to the jeweller,—and the diamond star that was the one thing she had to sell. Ah, that was between her and destitution. She started up. What had she done with it? She had been too utterly weary to think or care.

The draught was beating the dingy dividing curtain that swung on its iron rod; it bulged like a sail over the top of the chest of drawers, sweeping it clear; and it parted, giving a glimpse of a girl beyond with the star in her hands. She started.

"I was just putting it back," she said. "The curtain knocked it off on my side. How it sparkles!"

Susan stretched out her fingers, a little too eagerly.

"You needn't be so sharp," said the girl, disconcerted. "I could buy heaps like it for a shilling apiece at a shop in the Edgware Road," and she threw it back carelessly, and began to whistle to show she was not abashed.

She had a plain, good-humoured, impudent face and dusty hair. On her arms she wore a pair of black stockings with the feet cut off, fastened by safety pins to her under bodice. She was tying her petticoat.

"I want to sell this," said Susan. In her loneliness she was loth to offend a stranger.—"But I hope I shall get more than a shilling for it."

"I'll give you three," said the girl, and then was all at once smitten with awe. "I say—you don't mean to say it's real?"

Her off-hand manner became subdued; she looked curiously but respectfully at Susan.

"You came here unexpectedly, didn't you?" she said. "Did you know you had slept all Sunday? Mrs. White said you were dead tired, and that you were a lady. I'll lend you my brush, if you like;—and a bit of soap."

Susan smiled at this proof of confidence.

"I'll shut the window, shall I?" the girl went on, letting it slam as she withdrew the hair-brush. "I was airing my bed. I always make it before I go down because I'm anæmic, and I've no breath to run up all these flights of stairs after breakfast.— If you want to be private you can pull the curtain."

That was the one thing she would not willingly do for her; with her own hands shut out the view of one so mysterious.

The other sleepers were stirring behind their enshrouding folds, like hidden moths preparing to burst from the chrysalis. In one quarter after another the heavy breathing was cut short by an awaking sigh. One or two emerged with their jugs and padded barefoot to the hot-water tap on the landing.

"I'll get you a jugful, shall I?" said Susan's friend, and having installed herself as mistress of the ceremonies, returned to the subject of the star.

"Mind you don't try a pawnbroker," she said. "If you take my advice you'll walk into the swaggerest shop in Bond Street, where they are used to ladies."

"Why?" asked Susan.

The girl assumed a great air of worldly wisdom, cocking her head on one side like a London sparrow.

"Oh," she said, "*they* won't be so likely to lose their heads over you, and perhaps ask you how you got it."

She had not considered that. Her dismayed look gratified the girl, who at once adopted the manner of a protector.

CHAPTER XII

"You'll be all right," she said. "They'll know the difference in the Bond Street shops. It wouldn't do in the City."

*****

She had been in a jeweller's shop with Barnaby once, and it was in Bond Street. If she could find it ... the girl's suggestion had made her nervous; she would have more courage in going where she had been with him. Would they eye her askance even there? Would they make difficulties, ask questions? The thought harassed her.

She lingered a minute outside the shop, when she had found it; gazing into the glittering window, so preoccupied with her errand that it never entered her head that there might be anyone who would recognize her among the idle people that were abroad. Defending herself by a haughty carriage she took a long breath and went inside.

"How are you?"

She started as violently as if she had been a thief. She had never expected to meet this man again; and there he was, holding her limp hand in his.

"I saw you over the way," he said, "and plunged in here to catch you and ask about Barnaby. How is he getting on?"

At first she thought it must be in merciless irony he was speaking, and plucked up a spirit to defy him. He had glanced from her face to the counter; he was a witness of her singular transaction. She felt his glance burn her. What was he thinking of it?

"Oh, he is getting on very well," she said recklessly.

"Is he up here with you?" said Rackham. Was it possible that he did not know?—She gasped.

"No," she stammered. And now he looked at her more strangely. She was gathering up the price of her star and turning to leave the shop. They had made no demur; they had given her more than she dared to expect....

"Which way are you going?" said Rackham.

"Your way isn't mine," she said.

He was keeping at her side; she could not outstrip his strides with her flying little steps.

"But I want to talk to you," he said boldly. "You were a little beside yourself, weren't you, at our last meeting? I've not seen you since Barnaby's accident.... You blamed me for it, didn't you? My dear girl, if I had wanted to murder him I wouldn't have been so clumsy.—What are you doing in London all by yourself?"

That last question came suddenly, just when his bantering speech had roused her, and put her off her guard. He was watching her face; and it blanched.

"What's the trouble?" he said. "Confound—!"

He had cannoned into another man, whose approaching figure he had not marked. It was Kilgour, in London clothes, who blocked the way, with a growl for Rackham and a friendly hand-grip for Susan.

"Who's the man charging?" he grumbled. "Though you can't see daylight through me, still I'm not a bullfinch. Come along, Mrs. Barnaby; you are just the person I want. I've been praying my gods for a sympathetic eye. Come and look at my masterpiece in the window."

His large presence was a safeguard. She could have clung to him.

"Half Leicestershire is in Bond Street in a frost," he said. "I knew I'd run across somebody. I've been up myself since Friday. But what is Barnaby doing in town? What do the doctors say?"

What a fool she had been not to have dreaded this. Half Leicestershire in Bond Street! And she had fled to London, the great, engulfing city—! She could have laughed wildly at herself, at her childish want of precaution, her romantic imprudence in haunting places where she had been with him, where it was so likely that she would meet his acquaintances. But what would he think of her when he heard that she had been seen....?

Mechanically she walked on a few paces. Rackham was still at her right hand; he would not be shaken off. And Kilgour was talking in his loud, kind, friendly voice; taking it for granted that Barnaby and she were in town together. He did not guess that she was a runaway.

"It came to me in a vision on the top of Burrough Hill," he said. "Rain and mist and the setting sun.... A kind of greyish-black gauziness with a stripe of crimson. There! What do you think of that?"

With a grandiloquent gesture he pointed out a diminutive grey and black turban throned in solitary majesty in the middle of a shop-window. His shop; his personal achievement. A quaint pride sat on his good red face, roughened by wind and weather. It was somewhat akin to the pride great men feel in doing little things. The big successes in life are too overweighting; they oppress a man with the memory of his struggle, the long strain, the effort,—the troubling secret of how he has fallen short. Kilgour might have swelled with pride over greater matters, but when he thought of them he was humble.... He wagged a delighted forefinger at his creation, boasting.

"There isn't much of it," said Rackham.

Susan was between the two men; she felt like a caught bird that dared not flutter, and she had still a frantic desire to laugh.

"That's it," said Kilgour. "No feminine exaggeration. It's all idea and no trimming, instead of all trimmings and no idea. And as light as a feather. I tried it on myself."

She *was* laughing; not at the absurd image his speech called up, not at the picture of this bluff sportsman gravely regarding himself in a mirror, balancing his insecure idea on his close-cropped head;—but at the tragic absurdity of her own position. How little they knew, these men!

"Good-bye," she said. "I—I am in a hurry."

"Just wait a minute," said Kilgour. "There's another point in its favour. If you are in a hurry you can clap it on hind-before. Wait a bit and let me illustrate what I mean. Two or three doors up. You know this place? It's my rival *Jane*. Now, impartially, let's pick these hats to pieces."

But she interrupted his scientific disparagement rather wildly. She had not known how much she liked him, Barnaby's friend who might have talked to her of him if she had dared to loiter just for the sake of hearing his name spoken now and then.... She held out her hand to him wistfully.

"Good-bye, Lord Kilgour," she said hurriedly. "Good-bye!"

He squeezed the little hand kindly, not uttering his surprise till she had vanished from his ken.

"Bolted into the very shop!" he said. "How like a woman. Next time I meet her she'll have one of these monstrosities on her head."

He nodded carelessly at Rackham, to whom Susan had bidden no farewell, and strolled on, hailing his acquaintances, looking in the shops. Turning into Piccadilly he saw a face he knew coming towards him in a hansom, and raised his stick.

"Thought it was you," he said. "You don't look very fit to be out. What do you mean by it? I told your wife you had no business racketing in London."

The hansom had stopped. Barnaby was leaning out, staring at him.

"What did you say?" he asked. There was an incredulous eagerness in his voice.

"Eh?" said Kilgour, struck by his looks, and sorry. "Barnaby, old chap, you ought to be in bed. What's up? You haven't come to town to consult any fancy doctors? No complications, are there? It's generally when a fellow is mending that they crop up."

"No, it's not doctors," said Barnaby. "Look here, Kilgour——"

"Seems to me," said Kilgour, "as if you had been roped in by Christian Science. Don't you know what a battered-looking ghost you are?"

"I'm all right," said Barnaby impatiently. "Just answer me, Kilgour. What did you mean by saying you told my wife——?"

"I wasn't meddling," said Kilgour sagely, "I was offering a rational opinion——"

"Oh, stop fooling!" said Barnaby. "Do you mean you saw her?"

The other man was puzzled by the urgent note in his voice. Then he laughed.

"Missed her have you?" he said. "Oh, yes, you fractious invalid,—I saw her."

"When?"

There was no mistaking it. Barnaby was in earnest. For the second time Kilgour had a twinge, an uncomfortable recollection of a brown leather arm-chair in Wimpole Street and long white fingers handling one or two queer little scientific dodges that pried into hidden things. Once he had had to go with a friend. It had turned him sick, that minute or two of waiting in dead silence to hear the verdict.... Had Barnaby been there? ... He shook off the unwelcome fancy. If he knew anything of that girl she would not let Barnaby go into a lions' den without her.

"Half an hour ago," he said. "With your cousin in attendance. I met them coming out of What's-his-name's,—that jeweller's shop in Bond Street."

"What?" said Barnaby. He looked like a man whose wits were staggering under a mortal blow. Then his mouth set hard, in a fighting line.

"Bond Street," he called up the trap to the driver, and the hansom dashed jingling on. Kilgour was left marvelling on the kerb.

"By Jove!" he said to himself, proceeding to cool his perturbation in the peaceable atmosphere of his club, and stoutly refusing, though troubled in mind, to draw the inevitable conclusion.

CHAPTER XIII

Susan hardly knew how she reached the dreary place that was her refuge. Meeting Rackham had shaken her. An unaccountable restlessness took possession of her as she thought of him; she felt him pursuing her; she had an impulse to run and run until she was hidden from the penetrating intentness of his regard. In the shop whither she had fled she had tried to argue with herself, but it had been useless. The relief with which she had found herself for the moment free from him taught her too much.

She had glanced desperately backwards. He was not walking on with Kilgour.... What did she want; what excuse had she for staying till he was gone? She must buy something. Clothes for travelling;—was she not going to America?—and she had nothing, not even a handkerchief.

The suggestion steadied her. How soon could she sail? She must find out at once; must engage her passage.—They had nothing but hats in here, but an assistant directed her to another shop upstairs.

Recklessly,—since the prices here were extravagant prices for one who had only a handful of sovereigns between her and want,—she made purchases. It seemed to quiet her silly agitation, to restore to her something of her despairing calm.

But when she issued into the street again panic ruled her. She could not breathe freely until she was far from this dangerous neighbourhood, until at last she was shut inside the gloomy house in a side street, that barred out imaginary pursuers with the massive security of its blistered door.

But she must go out again; she must discover how quickly she could sail:— perhaps she was missing an opportunity.

The girl who had talked to her in the morning came in and brushed against her as she passed in the dim hall.

"Oh, it's you!" she said, stopping. "How dark it is in the passage! I wish they'd light the gas. How did you get on? I found something else of yours up there. It didn't look worth much, but it's no good leaving things about, and there isn't a key in your chest of drawers."

As she spoke she held out something.

"They've been talking about you," she went on, "saying things about you turning up at night without a bag or anything. They can't understand you calling yourself Miss and wearing a wedding ring. I told them it would be worse if you called yourself Mrs. and didn't. — You'll have to get some things, won't you?"

She looked inquisitively at Susan, who had sunk on to the hard wooden chair in the hall, unable to face the stairs. But the mysterious stranger was hardly attending to what she said, amounting as it did to a declaration that she had found a supporter. Lady Henrietta's unlucky brooch, that she had inadvertently taken with her, was just then a precious thing. She remembered how Barnaby had laughed at his mother, while she persisted in telling its history, and how she had vainly tried once or twice to throw it away, but had given up.

"I know it's bewitched," she had said.

"It is always bringing me small misfortunes, but I have an uncanny feeling that I mustn't part with it. Besides, I can't. It has fallen in the fire, and been left in a railway carriage, and had all kinds of mischances, but it has always come back to me. It's attached to me for ever and ever. I don't know what would break the spell."

Susan smiled a little as she gazed at that bit of dinted silver. Fate had made an end of the superstition. Surely she might keep it, valueless in itself, for the sake of the woman she would never see again. Its unluckiness did not matter....

"Yes," she said vaguely. "I must go and get some things."

What had the girl been saying? There was a kind of sympathy in her face.

"Would you come with me?" she asked, yielding to her instinctive need of companionship. She could not go out alone....

"Rather!" said the girl.

They set out, an ill-matched couple, flotsam that had drifted together, and would as casually drift apart. The Londoner led the way confidently, but surprised at Susan's first errand, the shipping office. It heightened her interest, and she listened closely to the stranger's eager inquiries. No, there was no room on the next boat sailing. She could have a berth in the following steamer if she liked, only three days later. But was there no boat to-morrow? — Oh, yes, but no cabin accommodation. The traveller did not care. She would go steerage.

"You're in a dreadful hurry to sail, aren't you?" said the Londoner, to whom the trip represented a tremendous voyage.

Yes, she was in a hurry.

"And you keep so close to me; you turn your head sometimes as if you thought we were followed. What are you afraid of?"

Susan tried to smile, but the truth was too near her lips.

"A man," she said nervously, with her thoughts on Rackham.

The other seemed to understand. She did not ask any more questions, but was kind and useful, advising her, helping her, reminding her that she must buy a trunk. Till they turned the last corner, and were within a few yards of the Rabbit Warren, as this old inhabitant called the house; then she hung back a little, glancing right and left.

CHAPTER XIII 121

"You're not quite yourself, are you?" she said, consideringly. Her eyes had the brightened gleam of one plunging alive into a serial tale, one of these in which lords and ladies behave strangely and the typewriting girl rules the tempest. As she put her key in the latch she looked round again. But there were no untoward appearances dogging them in the distance. There was a disappointing emptiness in the street.

The gas was lit in the hall at last, accentuating its gloom. The rather dismal illumination fell on a mahogany table under the stair where stood a row of candlesticks, each bearing a different length of candle and a slip of paper.

Susan's ally paused to examine them, reading out the names scribbled on the slips. It was the custom for those who were to be out late to leave their candles in the hall, and the last one in, finding a solitary candlestick left downstairs, knew that it was her business to chain the door.

"Miss Shanklin, Miss Friend, Miss Mitchell—" read out the inquisitor. "Mitchell is burnt down into the socket; she reads in bed. She'll set us on fire one night.— Miss Robinson—that's me, but I've changed my mind:—Miss Grahame—"

Susan made no sign. Then she remembered.—That was her name again.

"Oh, yes," she said, "is that mine?"

The other girl nodded to herself.

"Well," she said. "It's been brought down by mistake. Better take it up with you; they don't turn the gas off till ten."

She watched Susan go wearily up the long flights, and then ran swiftly along the passage and called down to the basement. The boy who opened the door to strangers and carried coals answered her call out of the black gulf of the kitchen stair;—his eyes glittering, like a demon invisible in the dark.

"What are you ladies wanting now?" he asked in an injured voice—"You can't have 'em!"

"Gerald," said the girl mysteriously, "come up. Higher;—higher! If anybody calls here asking for a lady, darkish, with grey eyes, and middling tall,—never mind what name he says—! Don't breathe a word of it, but fetch me."

"Doesn't sound like you," said Gerald, but grinned, diving backwards into his native gloom.

Miss Robinson turned from the basement stairs and began her long journey to the top of the house. No, wild horses would not drag her out that night. Did they always write down a traveller's address at the shipping office? Supposing it were her lot to draw two sundered hearts together?

The Rabbit Warren was a depressing house. As the day waned its dreariness increased; it grew fuller of tired women whose search for work had been useless, and who came trudging in with the twilight to join the rest who had been listening all day with straining ears for the postman, while they studied ceaselessly the advertisement sheets in the daily paper.

It was chiefly the incapable, the discouraged, those who had fallen out of the ranks through ill health, or were losing their hold because they were not any longer young, who drifted into this harbour. They were all in a manner waifs, and they had nothing to hope for but that they might die in harness.

Susan sat with her cheek on her hand, withdrawn a little, in the dingy sitting room. She was unconscious of the whispering interest she excited; she did not hear the subdued discussion that raged around her. But the atmosphere of the house weighed on her, charged as it was with failure. It was robbing her of courage.

How strange it was to look back; almost unbearable. How hard it was to look forward. She was to sail to-morrow ... she must be brave....

The girl who had struck up a casual alliance with her sat amidst the others, ripping the ragged binding off a skirt. Her sallow face was less heavy than usual, her eyes alight.

She had glanced up quickly as Susan came in, and had begun to hum a tune, snipping fast. It had been impossible to resist the temptation to crystallise wandering speculation and focus the general attention for awhile on herself by a few dark hints and thereupon thrilling silence. The rest fell with a pathetic eagerness on the brief distraction that lightened their dreary lives. They had outlived their own little histories; no excitement touched any of them but the recurrent terror of wanting bread.

All at once Miss Robinson laid down her scissors and listened intently to something she heard without.

"Is that coals?" said one, huddling near the fire, in a hushed voice, as who should say—Might the Gods relent?—But no full scuttle bumped the panels as Gerald put in his head.

"Wanted," he said, and grinned.

Miss Robinson gave one gasp, half in fright, half triumphant, and fled out of the room, shutting the door with care.

Then, for a moment, cowardice nearly quenched her long-unslaked thirst for drama. Visions of herself as mediatrix, restoring a runaway wife to her frantic husband, were upset by fearful misgivings in which she saw herself figuring, not in the gilded realm of the serial page, but in lurid paragraphs on the other side of the paper. Paragraphs in which someone heard pistol-shots....

In the dim passage she clutched at Gerald.

"What is he like?" she whispered.

"A regular toff," said Gerald in an awed voice. "Asked for a Miss Grant. None of that name here.—Slight, dark lady.—And then I twigged that he was your party. I've seen his picture once in the *News of the World*; they snapped him, held up by the police in his motor. How did you get to know 'im, Miss Robinson? He's a lord."

"Oh!" she said. This was indeed a sensation. This would last her all her life!—

CHAPTER XIII

*****

Barnaby had had no luck in Bond Street.

He sat forward in his hansom, leaning out, gripping the front, ready to dash it open. It did not matter to him how many fools were about, how many frivolous idiots, men and women, stopped short in their idle progress and stared at him. Down Old Bond Street, along New Bond Street, right to the end he went, raking the narrow thoroughfare with a searching gaze. The shop signs mocked him. Milliners, jewellers, palmists, druggists, picture-sellers: a fantastic jumble. She might be anywhere, within two or three yards of him, and he not know it. She might have just gone in at that door yonder that was closing. She might be just coming out.

Half an hour ago. One chance in a hundred.... More likely she was miles off, whizzing in one of these cursed taxis—!

Well, he could hunt down Rackham. He would drive to that old barrack of his in Marylebone. No,—that was let or shut up or something. Where the devil did he go when he was in town?

It was late in the afternoon before he ran him down. He had been heard of, or seen, in most of his ordinary haunts. One man had come across him in a saddler's shop, another had passed him ten minutes ago in the Haymarket. And at last Barnaby found him coming out of his tailors'. He stopped the hansom.

"Get in," he said.

"Hullo!" said Rackham, staring at him. "What's wrong with you?" But he obeyed mechanically, and the hansom started off. "What d'you mean by kidnapping a fellow like this? Where on earth are we going?"

"I've told him to drive to my hotel," said Barnaby curtly. There was a controlled fury in his voice.

"But why the deuce——"

"I'm not going to have a row in a cab."

"Whew!" said Rackham, twisting round and regarding the grim outline of his cousin's profile, his stubbornly closed mouth. Unless Barnaby were stark mad there was something serious in the wind, something he could not trust himself to utter without losing his hold on himself.

It was not far to the hotel. Barnaby got out stiffly and Rackham followed.

"I hope you've got a nurse on the premises," he said,—"or a keeper."

"We'll go to my room," said Barnaby, in the same deadly quiet voice. Up there he closed the door and turned round on Rackham like one who had got to the end of his tether.

"Now!" he said. "Damn you, what have you done with my wife?"

"What?" said Rackham. He had not expected that charge.

"You know where she is," said Barnaby. "Don't lie to me. You were with her in Bond Street——"

So that was it.

"How should I know if you don't?" said Rackham. "Do you mean she's gone?"

His eagerness was unmistakable. It was worth a torrent of empty protestation. The two men looked each other straight in the eyes.

The likeness between them came out then, when they were roused. Something in the angry set of the jaw, something in their expression; a recklessness, a hard blue stare.

Barnaby had dropped his stick. He could stand up without its support. For the time he had borrowed strength of passion.

"You don't know?" he said, and took a long breath.

"I don't," said Rackham. "There's no occasion to fight me, if that's what you brought me here for. I saw her; I spoke to her;—but I was fool enough not to understand. I supposed she was up in town for the day, buying rubbish. I never doubted she was going back.—I thought you were still on your sick-bed and she was looking after you—"

He checked himself abruptly in the burst of angry candour that his surprise evoked.

"You needn't look so damnably glad—" he broke out, "because I've shown myself a simpleton, not a villain. Look here, Barnaby, I've answered your question. I'll ask you to tell me one thing. She's gone, and you have lost her. What do you mean to do?"

"Search London from end to end," said Barnaby, "till I find her."

"That's how we stand, is it?" said Rackham. "You're not wise enough to let her go?"

He spoke more slowly, recovering from his astonishment. There was a light in his eye, and into his voice had come a ring of exultation. He had got over his first vexation, his rage at his own stupid failure to guess the great good news.

"What right have you to say that?" cried Barnaby.

"For the matter of that," said Rackham, "what rights have you?"

The shot told. For a minute they looked again fixedly at each other.

"You had my answer," said Barnaby, "when I spoke of her as my wife."

"You stick to that then?" said Rackham. "Though she has found it unsupportable, though she's gone—you still hold to that pretence? What's the good? You don't care a straw for the girl. Oh, I've seen you together; I know the terms you were on.—It's sheer obstinacy makes you play the dog-in-the-manger——"

"Take care," said Barnaby, breathing hard.

"Let's drop that humbug," said Rackham. "*I'm* no gossip.—But I've had an inkling from the first. I've guessed all along that it was a plant of your mother's.—Infernally inconvenient of you to turn up and spoil it—! But I held my tongue. Nobody else had any idea of how the land lay but Julia.—There's a devilish instinct sometimes in a jealous woman—"

He laughed shortly. Something in Barnaby's look amused him.

"What? She's been reproaching you, has she, after all?" he said. "Well, I did you one service there. If I hadn't kept her quiet, she'd have shrieked it all out on the house-tops on the night of the Melton Ball. You owe me something for that, Barnaby. There 'ud always have been a few who wouldn't have put her down as a raving lunatic. Mind, I didn't muzzle her for your sake—I did that for Susan. I wasn't going to stand by and see that woman hounding 'em on—!"

"Have you done?" said Barnaby. He had got back some measure of self-control.

"I'm done if you are reasonable," said Rackham. "Why not own up and tell me what you can, and let me look for her. I swear I'll find her—but not for you."

Barnaby took one step towards him, and he stood back quickly, smiling at his own involuntary precaution. He could afford to smile, to stave off a scuffle that would summon all the rabble in the hotel.

"Steady!" he said. "Don't try to kill me. It would be a waste of time for both of us. I'm not afraid of you, Barnaby, but I have something else to do,—now,—than to stop rowing up here with you. I'd better warn you—"

Barnaby was struggling to hold himself in. Susan had still to be found, and she would want his protection. Rackham was right there, damn him; he must not lose his head.

"And I warn *you*," he said. "I'll find my wife without your help. Do you hear what I say?—my wife, Rackham. I don't care what story you have got hold of. Understand that. She belongs to me."

"And yet she's gone," said Rackham.

Somebody was knocking at the door, but so discreetly that neither of the two men heard. Rackham, turning to go, had halted to fling back his taunting word. And the other man had no answer. His own storming haste had undone him.

"You can't get over that, can you?" said Rackham. "It knocks the bottom out of your doggedness. If she doesn't choose to carry it on you can do nothing."

"I can take care of her," said Barnaby. His voice sounded hoarse.

"No, you can't," said Rackham, with a sudden fierceness that matched his own. "That will be my business."

"Yours?" said Barnaby, and his look was dangerous. He advanced on the other man with a clenching hand.

"Because," said Rackham, "if she's not your wife:—and she's not; she's nothing to you—I shall make her mine."

In the short silence that fell between them the knocking became insistent.

"Better let them in," said Rackham, "I'm going."

Barnaby pulled himself together and turned the key. His locking the door had been an instinctive action. And Rackham passed out, ignoring the insignificant person waiting on the threshold, who met Barnaby's look of blank interrogation with an apologetic reminder of his own orders. He had said if a message came it was to be brought up at once. And a message it was;—from the shipping office.

*****

Rackham swung out of the place like a conqueror. The knowledge that Susan had run away was to him the knowledge that he had won.

He never doubted that he would find her, and inspiration helped him, as it will the man whose blood runs quicker under the stimulus of his belief in his luck. What was the shop she had flown into to escape him and Kilgour, and the embarrassment of their ignorant questions? He had stayed long enough outside to know it again, waiting till he had no excuse for loitering any longer. She must have made purchases. He went straight there.

How simple it was, with luck on his side, to call in and say that a lady who had been that morning was afraid she had forgotten to leave her name and address.... This was no big emporium, but a little exclusive shop where it was possible to describe a customer's appearance with a chance of finding it remembered by saleswomen who recognized his standing and were sympathetically amused. In the hat-shop they directed him upstairs, and there he found an equal appreciation of his attitude of comical despair, as he tried helplessly to run through a list of feminine furbelows that the careless lady was supposed to have ordered to be sent home. How should a man succeed?—Smiling they reassured him. They recollected the lady perfectly from his description, and she had made no mistake in that establishment; the parcel was already packed and waiting to be despatched. To satisfy him an assistant was bidden to read out the address on the label, and as she glanced up at him, expecting him to verify it, Rackham checked himself just in time. For the name she slurred over was strange to him.

Why, he had thought of that,—since naturally the runaway was no longer masquerading as his cousin's wife;—and yet he had been about to deny that it was she. What had it sounded like? Grant, or Grand?—And was it indeed Susan, or a stranger? He had no means of knowing; the only thing possible was to go blindly forward, trusting in his luck and fixing that address in his head.

"Yes, yes, that's all right," he acknowledged, and laughed good-naturedly at the apparent futility of his mission as he sauntered out of the shop.

*****

It was Miss Robinson's mysterious signal that cleared the room. One by one, like startled shadows, its denizens flitted thence, and left Rackham alone with Susan.

They hung over the stairs, buzzing like bees in the semi-darkness, thrilled by an interest that was vaguely heightened by alarm. At intervals they hushed each other into silence, listening with bated breath lest anything might transpire, and watching with a kind of fascination the crack of light that issued from the door of the sitting room. Only Miss Robinson herself went whispering, whispering on.

CHAPTER XIII

"Poor little girl!" said Rackham.

There was triumph and pity and a threatening kindness in his voice. His reckless personality seemed to fill the room that had been so suddenly deserted.

She had risen to her feet with a gasp at his entrance. A wave of panic swept over her head and left her slightly trembling;—because she had had no warning.

"How did you come here?" she said.

"Oh," he said, smiling down upon her. "I prevailed on a drab young woman who seems to have constituted herself your guardian to bring me in. I wasn't going to risk your giving me the slip as you did this morning. You wouldn't have seen me if I'd sent in a ceremonious message."

"No," she said, "I would not."

"I knew that," said Rackham. "The same pride that kept you from telling me the truth would have hidden you from me. You'd have had me turned from the door.—But the drab romancer was a great ally, though I've had to agree with most of her wild surmises.—I'll make you forgive me later."

He laughed under his breath.

"She asked me," he said, "if I was your husband."

"You—you—! Did you let her think——" cried Susan in a choking voice, fighting against a strange sense of the inevitable that his look inspired.

"Oh, she had been thinking hard," he said. "A runaway stranger, calling herself Miss—Grahame, was it?—I got it wrong—and wearing a wedding ring. What more likely—? I had the part thrust on me directly I showed my face."

He dropped the half-jesting air that had masked his excitement, and came nearer. She shivered a little at his approach.

"Daren't you trust me, Susan?" he said. "I'm not a Pharisee.—Why, I guessed it from the beginning. Don't you remember how I asked you to let me help you if you wanted a friend?—And all the while I was watching. Do you think I can't guess how Barnaby drove his bargain, careless of you, trading on your helplessness in the shock of his return? What did he care that it was hard on you, so long as it suited his selfish purpose?"

"He was good to me," she said. It was no use denying anything any more.

"Are you grateful to him—still?" said Rackham.

She turned away her face.

Something in her attitude kindled in him that instinct of protection that had from the first struggled in his soul with admiration. Had he not felt a consuming rage that it had not been his to battle for her, to turn round on Barnaby and his world, all pointing the finger of scorn at her for a cheat?—He would have liked them to do their worst, would have liked to defy them.... Well, that occasion was his at last.

Barnaby had nearly fooled him. The extraordinary course he had taken had at first made Rackham curse himself for an imaginative ass. But he had been right. His time had come.... And Barnaby was defeated.

"Well," he said, "that's ended. I'll take care of you now, I'll take you out of this. Look at me! There's nothing between us now, no fictitious barrier, no mistaken idea of loyalty to a man who took advantage of your false step to make you play his own foolish game. You made a gallant show. It almost deceived me, once or twice, almost made me believe you liked him.... Never mind that. Like a brave girl you've freed yourself from that intolerable position. And I'm here, Susan, where I always was, at your feet."

She lifted her head; a little, sad, desperate face upturned.

"Why must you insult me?" she said. "Is it because I am all alone?"

"I'm asking you to marry me," said Rackham.

She stared at him for a minute. His pursuit of her was not all selfish: there was an impatient fondness in his reckless face.

"I—?" she said faintly. "A woman of whom you know nothing but that she came among you as an impostor? You cannot mean what you say, Lord Rackham."

He broke in on her protestation roughly.

"Do you think I mind tattle?" he said. "Let their tongues wag. We'll hold up our heads and flout 'em. I'll leave it to Barnaby to find a way out of his muddle.— Lord, how it will puzzle them,—how they'll jabber when they see our marriage advertised in the *Morning Post*—!"

He was taking her assent for granted, arrogant in the heat of his headlong moment. Perhaps it did not strike him as possible that she would refuse. What woman in her plight would not lean gladly on the rescuer who came to offer her his kingdom? Perhaps he was blinded by his confidence in his luck.

"I—can't marry you!" she said.

Rackham did not fall back. He laughed indulgently. Was she troubled because of the world's opinion?

"Dear, silly child," he said. "Don't be frightened. I'll make them treat you properly. I'll make them swallow their amazement; and they shall be kind to you."

Yes, this man loved her. That was why she was afraid of him. She was not used to being loved like that. She had never learned to see in it help, instead of danger....

"I can't marry you," she repeated, but her breath came fast.

"Oh, but you must!" he said. "Fate is on my side. What kind of a struggle can you make against me all by yourself? I've found you, Susan, and I'll never let you go.... There's nothing too outrageous for me to undertake, and nothing on earth to stop me.—Your hands are trembling."

He bent to seize them in his, brushing aside her mute defiance with his violent tenderness, as determined as Fate itself. Just for a minute she felt very tired in spirit, very weak to resist him. It was so strange, although it was terrible, to be loved.

CHAPTER XIII

Why should any man care so deeply as to stand between her and the emptiness of the world? Might she not, if she submitted, find the strange worship sweet?

She did not know she was wavering until she understood his smile, and with that her heart was smitten by a fugitive likeness, a trick of manner, reminding her of another man. Uselessly, poignantly, memory stabbed her. She flung out these trembling hands.

"No!" she panted. The thought of it was unbearable. "I can't—I can't!"

He was taken aback by the vehemence of her cry. For a moment he did not speak, looking at her queerly. His laugh was angry.

"I've a great mind to bundle you into a cab and carry you off," he said. "Oh, they'd let me!—I've only to tell these people that you are my wife and a little mad. My tale would sound more probable than yours."

She was not sure that he was not in earnest. Panic-stricken she shook off his hold on her arm, meaning to pass him and reach the door. Why?—To make a futile bid for sympathy in this house of strangers?—

Who was it that had turned the handle and was coming in? Her gaze was unbelieving; she could neither breathe nor stir till the suffocating leap of her heart assured her that it was true. For it was Barnaby himself who was standing in the doorway, just as he had stood on that night when she had seen him first. Only the look in his eyes was changed.

The same faintness overcame her that had stricken her down that night. She did not know whose arms had caught her as she was falling ... falling.... But she was afraid of nothing, though all was darkness.

"Your race, Barnaby," said Rackham.

CHAPTER XIV

"I knew we should get you back," said Lady Henrietta.

That had been her first word last night, and she repeated it with the emphasis of a prophetess justified. Still her clasp of the truant had been almost fierce.

The journey to London had done her no harm. Rather had all this excitement given her a fillip. There was a triumphant pink in her cheek, and amusement twinkled in the fine lines surrounding the corners of her eyes. Whilst Barnaby had been searching she had been busy, dealing with an imposing but worldly personage in gaiters, who had been an old admirer of hers and was her sworn ally. The situation charmed her; it was like a thrilling but perfectly righteous bit of intrigue. Quizzically, delightedly, she was regarding Susan.

"Yes," she maintained. "I pinned my faith to that battered old brooch of mine. It's unlucky to wear, but still—when I remembered that it was doomed to come back to me I was tranquil. I knew it would."

She turned from one to the other, challenging them to mock at her superstition; and then she laughed.

"My dear!" she said. "I'll never forget his face when I was raging at him.—I blamed him, you may be sure. Or his voice when he called to me—'She has written!' I could get no more out of him till I lost my patience and cried—'Then for Heaven's sake read the letter and tell me what she says!' And when he said—'She says she has found out that my marriage was illegal' I could only exclaim—'Thank goodness!'"

She laughed again at her picture of his amazement.

"I shocked him awfully," she said. "But I was transported. It had solved a riddle.... 'So *that* was the mysterious American business,' I said, '*that* is what was the matter! And she has rushed off and set you free and all the rest of it, you undeserving laggard! If that's all it can soon be mended.'—And then he woke up from his stupefaction. But it was I who thought of the Bishop. It was I who suggested a special licence. I am the head conspirator, Susan,—and I'll go and put on my things."

She went, glancing back to them as she reached the door.

"Don't let her out of your sight, Barnaby," she said warningly, and left them together.

The girl stayed where she was, quite still; gazing down from the dizzy height of the window on the restless world in the streets below. Barnaby was limping across to her side. She felt his touch on her shoulder.

CHAPTER XIV 131

"There's the church down there," he said. "Like an island in a whirlpool, isn't it? But all the roar and the rush dies down like the noise in a dream when you get inside. It's wonderfully dim and dark in there, and they're dusting the pews for us,—and there are a few lilies on the altar. And we'll just walk into it hand in hand."

Her breath came hurriedly, like a sob.

"Are you—sure?" she said.

"Ah," he reminded her, "I've never made love to you, have I, Susan?"

She could not answer him, knowing him so close; and she dared not look up at him. There was so much to remember, and she had begun to guess how dangerous it had been.... He laughed, and his hand leaned heavier on her shoulder.

"I've been hopping all over London like a mad cripple," he said, "and at last I've got you. I must hold on to you, or you'll manage to disappear. Why did you run away when you thought I couldn't follow? It wasn't fair. Oh, my darling, couldn't you understand?"

His voice was not steady now; there was reproach in its passionate undertone.

"I'm sorry," she said, and laid her cheek against his sleeve. This thing that was still too wonderful was true.

"Why," said Barnaby. "It was only you from the first,—that first night when the sight of you staggered me. I didn't know why, but I did know that at any cost, at any risk, I couldn't let you go. I thought I was strong enough, man enough, to keep you safe in my house:—and when I began to find out what a hard thing I had undertaken, when I had to fight back the mad desire to make the farce we played at real,—you believed that I had betrayed you to another woman.... I've got your letter, your dear scrap of a piteous letter, letting me know that she and I had no barrier between us.... And that was to be the last I heard of you, was it, Susan?"

The reproach in his question was lost in its bantering tenderness.

"Wait," he said, "till I have you safe, and I'll teach you... And then, perhaps, we'll dare to look back on it all and laugh,—a long time afterwards; just you and I, by ourselves."

Lady Henrietta was back already. She had been discreet, had asked for no fuller explanation than the one she had so promptly furnished herself. It was all she was to know; but she was too wise to pry. At the back of her mind there was nothing but an absolute satisfaction, as of a warrior who had won her battle. If her eyes, shrewd and understanding, were dimmed a little as she considered them, she flung off her emotion quickly and smiled again.

"How funny it is," she said. "You have no idea how I am enjoying myself, you children. Put her furs on, Barnaby, button her up to the chin. I promised the Bishop we wouldn't be late. Secret marriages never are."

Then, hurrying him, she was moved to plague him with an irrepressible spark of mischief.

"Incomprehensible pair," she said. "I wish I had been at your first wedding. It must have been frightfully romantic."

Barnaby put away his watch. An unconquerable flicker lit up his eyes.

"It was," he said. "I just took her hand like this, and I said—" he was holding it tight in his—"Let's go and get married, Susan."

Lector House believes that a society develops through a two-fold approach of continuous learning and adaptation, which is derived from the study of classic literary works spread across the historic timeline of literature records. Therefore, we aim at reviving, repairing and redeveloping all those inaccessible or damaged but historically as well as culturally important literature across subjects so that the future generations may have an opportunity to study and learn from past works to embark upon a journey of creating a better future.

This book is a result of an effort made by Lector House towards making a contribution to the preservation and repair of original ancient works which might hold historical significance to the approach of continuous learning across subjects.

HAPPY READING & LEARNING!

LECTOR HOUSE LLP
E-MAIL: lectorpublishing@gmail.com

www.ingramcontent.com/pod-product-compliance
Lightning Source LLC
LaVergne TN
LVHW041604070526
838199LV00049B/2135